The Anathema Stone

by the same author

DEATH OF AN ALDERMAN
DEATH IN MIDWINTER
HANGMAN'S TIDE
NO BIRDS SANG
RESCUE FROM THE ROSE
GAMEKEEPER'S GALLOWS
DEAD-NETTLE
SOME RUN CROOKED

non-fiction

THE LANGUAGE LABORATORY IN SCHOOL
LANGUAGE TEACHING: A SYSTEMS APPROACH

JOHN BUXTON HILTON

The
Anathema Stone

ST. MARTIN'S PRESS
NEW YORK

Library of Congress Cataloging in Publication Data

Hilton, John Buxton.
  The anathema stone.

  I. Title.
PZ4.H6568An 1980   [PR6058.I5]   823'.9'14   79-25352
ISBN 0-312-03351-6

For
Ryan and Miranda
whose hospitality,
patience
and
patio
enabled this book
to be licked into shape

Part One

CHAPTER I

It can be a lovely month, October –

People had commiserated cheerfully when this year's holiday had had to be put off. Everything had seemed to take precedence over the Kenworthys' private life: a court case, an internal inquisition, even other men's inflexible leave arrangements. Then Simon had made the suggestion, outrageous on his lips, that he would rather like to see Derbyshire again. Twice he had had cases in the High Peak, each time had come back with a Londoner's contempt for the primitive, and an exaggerated relish for suburban comforts. For her part, Elspeth had not been averse to a journey north. She could see herself enjoying high and empty hills.

The air's so serene in October. You get the most marvellous views.

She had insisted on self-catering; hotel life would get her down in three days. And she knew what Simon was like in a residents' lounge. There was a cottage to rent in the columns of the *Observer;* the village of Spentlow was an unknown quantity, but its position on the map seemed just right: it was a small place, some 600 on the electoral roll, which, with youngsters and visitors, kept the population at about the thousand mark. According to the County Guide, a start had been made in the late 1950s to build a speculative estate on one of its flanks, but the project had not reached more than about a dozen desirable residences.

Then, somewhere along the climb into limestone country, something parted at the business end of the prop-shaft, doing untold damage to the rusted cross-members, and fatigue of metal became temporarily more relevant than fatigue of a mere Detective-Superintendent. If the garage lived up to its promises the car would be on the road again in time for the drive home. Meanwhile, there not being enough in the kitty for a hire car, they took a taxi up to Spentlow and peeled off their wet clothing.

For in October it can also rain. It was raining when the prop-shaft went, raining throughout the two-mile walk to the call-box. Rain sluiced down the streets of grey stone towns and obscured the empty hills. Rain sheeted across Spentlow Green like something from the effects department of the early cinema. Yet Kenworthy did not seem to mind. The serenity so deficient from the October skies appeared to have transferred itself to his outlook. He had brought only three books with him and the first of these, a lesser-known Trollope, seemed to be holding him like a charm.

Elspeth kept her fingers crossed. She had two main fears: the first, that he would become bored; the second, its corollary, that he would get himself involved in something. There was something tantalizing in his apparent failure to do either. He raised his eyes only occasionally from *He Knew He Was Right,* and that only to charge his pipe. She had almost to drive him from the house while she cooked their first supper; the cottage ran only to a living-room kitchen and she had to get him off her skyline while she deployed, an exercise in elimination, the various rusty egg-whisks, gnawed spatulas and charred-bottomed pans that were on the inventory.

There were two pubs, Kenworthy discovered, and they sliced across the sub-cultures of Spentlow as keenly as a cheese-wire. The Pack Horse, on the outskirts, was a triumph of brewer's fancy, with plastic-topped tables and contemporary mirrors advertising forgotten brews.

Its customers were mostly executives from Allsop Close who commuted to Derby, Manchester and Sheffield: immaculate blue denim from Adam's apple to ankle, and Fu Manchu moustaches. The licensee, John Allsop, stood in such close and satisfied relationship with them that he managed to serve Kenworthy without appearing to notice him.

In the village centre, on the other hand, the Recruiting Sergeant had Edwardian frosted windows, flaking plaster and a urinal swimming in Jeyes Fluid. It had clients with yellow teeth; ale was delivered by gravity from a firkin barrel on wooden trestles; and the landlord, one Billy Brightmore, winked at Kenworthy every time one of his customers said something monstrously uninformed, which happened roughly four times a minute. Kenworthy withdrew modestly downstage and settled down to sip unobtrusively.

He was used to the vapour of talk that rose round him whenever he moved among men who had just whispered to each other who he was, but there was one drinker who nodded to him with the affability of a member of the establishment spotting a peer: a man some ten years older than himself, early fifties, a gaunt figure, standing by the bar in pale corduroys and a heavily- though neatly-darned khaki pullover. Strange how retired officers of field rank are so equitably scattered about the English countryside. Maybe their ultimate pastures are assigned to them when they first enter Sandhurst.

'It shows how pushed we are for talent,' the Colonel was saying. 'I told the padre that I hadn't trodden the boards since I was second broker's man in a cadet pantomime.'

'And they've made you Mr Gabbitas, haven't they?' someone asked. 'That ought to give you some scope.'

'It will if I remember any of my words on the night.'

Then Kenworthy saw the poster with its amateur lettering:

SPENTLOW ST GILES
Rev. Wilbur Gabbitas
Centenary

'Big event in the village, I see.'

'Yes, what with the play and a book that the vicar has written. And Mr Dunderdale – he says – '

'Yes? What does Mr Dunderdale say? Name-dropping again, are we, Charlie?'

The thunder came from the depths of a black beard that had appeared in the doorway, surmounting a pyramid of cloak and cape that was fixed across the speaker's throat with a metal chain; not so much a man as a monument, and not so much a monument as a presence, which owed something, but not all, to his antique garb and fecundity of whisker. Stripped of theatricality, the man would still have stood six foot seven and had a nine-gallon ribcage.

'Evening, Vicar.'

A pint in pewter was being drawn without his need to speak an order. The Reverend Dunderdale weighed up the gathering and came and sat beside Kenworthy, pointedly leaving his beer unacknowledged.

'Pleased to meet you. The news has travelled fast, of course, that you are from Scotland Yard. And there are theories as to what you are doing here.'

'Resting.'

'If you ask us to believe that, then of course we shall. Well, if the rain continues and you are sufficiently bored by Sunday to seek the entertainment of matins, you might try resting in one of our pews. I dare say someone will squeeze up to make room for you.'

He crossed to his pint. Kenworthy studied the rest of the poster. A week was to be devoted to the memory of the nineteenth-century cleric: on the Monday evening, a lantern lecture on 'Bygone Spentlow' by the Reverend Daniel Dunderdale. On the Friday and Saturday nights, a play in the Village Hall, *The Anathema Stone: Scenes from the Life of Wilbur Gabbitas*, by Daniel Dunderdale. Throughout the week there would be on sale *The Second Book of Hob: Unpublished Papers by Wilbur Gabbitas*, edited by Daniel Dunderdale. And there was to be a charity auction: gifts of 'bygones' gratefully received; all profits to the Belfry Fund.

Leaning with his back to the bar, the vicar followed Kenworthy's interest.

'How long are you staying, Mr Kenworthy?'

'Three weeks.'

'Lucky man. You'll be able to see it all. Buy a book; buy several books. Stock up with Christmas presents.'

'Your man Gabbitas – bit of a lad, was he?'

'Well, he wasn't a Parson Woodforde or a Kilvert, but we think he had his points. Some of us believe he deserves a wider public than he has. He's going to get one, too, isn't he?'

This was addressed to the public at large, but each man left his neighbour to respond. Dunderdale's enthusiasms were evidently tolerated rather than shared.

'And I am reminded, Arthur Brightmore, that your name is not on the subscription list.' They all seemed to be Brightmores in this pub.

'Well, now, Vicar: two pounds. That's a lot of money for a book.'

'It may *seem* a lot of money. But you can't *not* buy one, Arthur. After all, you're *in* it.'

'I don't see how I can be in it. Mr Gabbitas died thirty years before I was born.'

'Ah, but he foresaw you, Arthur. He foresaw you.'

And Arthur started having his leg pulled.

'I reckon there'll be the tale about that time you were courting Sarah Anne Mycock, and you fixed it so you both got punctures. Only she had a repair outfit in her handbag.'

'You mean you've updated the *Tales*, like?' Arthur asked.

And Daniel Dunderdale laughed enormously, with the sort of mischief that might on occasion lose its sense of responsibility.

'Updated them, like,' he agreed.

They were interrupted by the door opening again, only this time it flew inwards, as if its handle had been torn from someone's grasp. Rain and autumn leaves swirled in from an impenetrable black backcloth. A couple came in, and the door was secured again, pro-ducing a renewed era of calm that suggested that the pub was sealed off from the outside world.

The man was one of those who would have been well advised not to let his hair grow long. It hung about his shoulders in a lank curtain, and was held against his ears by a sodden velvet band. His companion, like himself in her mid-twenties, had hair that had been reduced by the weather to the texture of boiled string. She was wearing an ankle-length dress in patchwork of pragmatic design over army surplus boots, and about her shoulders a tweed sports-jacket of nineteen-thirties' cut, its sleeves hanging empty. Even odder than the appearance of the pair was the fact that they seemed not merely tolerated here, but positively respected.

'Good evening, John. Good evening, Christine.'

The vicar could not have treated them with greater dignity if they had personally underwritten every bell in his tower. Labourers and veterans all nodded to them, and even the Colonel raised his hand in acknowledgement. Shortly afterwards, he and the vicar left together, the Colonel saying that he must tidy himself up for parade. There was perceptible relief from tension when the great cloak had swirled out into the storm.

'If you ask me, the Reverend Gabbitas never left any papers. What's in that book has come out of Dunderdale's head.'

'I'm buggered if I'm going to pay two quid for one.'

'I shall. I wouldn't miss it for a small fortune.'

'He'll end up landing himself in a court case.'

'Who'd go to court, and get ten times as much publicity?'

'Jesse Allsop might.'

'He'll leave Jesse Allsop alone. He'll make it look as if he's having a go, but there'll be nothing in it. Nobody's going to tell the truth about the Allsops.'

'Nobody *knows* the bloody truth about the Allsops.'

'Funny, though, nothing's been said about that cloak-tree.'

'Yet.'

'Nothing will.'

'The vicar's not said a dicky-bird.'

'He's biding his time.'

'So's Jesse Allsop.'

'Pity it had to go to the printer so soon. He could have made something out of these Beaker Folk.'

'And that big ginger Irishman. What was his name? Kevin O'Shea. And the girl.'

'One or two others and the girl.'

'It was all written before the girl was fairly out of the cradle. She's come on a lot, these last few months, that girl has.'

'You can say that again.'

Someone nudged the last speaker's elbow, reminding him of the presence of the hippy pair. Silence fell over the company for seconds, yet the couple did not seem to have heard the conversation, so immersed they were in their talk. Kenworthy caught the words 'Kantian' and 'transcendental significance'.

The story of the cloak-tree emerged obliquely from the dialogue that followed. A week ago, Jesse Allsop had sent over from Dogtooth Farm to the Village Hall an article of furniture for sale in the Mock Auction in connection with

the Gabbitas celebrations. Not jumble: the vicar had let
it be known that he wanted good stuff. And by all
accounts he was getting it, including this mid-
eighteenth-century coat- and hat-stand in mellowed
mahogany, 'Worth a blooming fortune,' a man in a
knotted neck-scarf said, that had been in the Allsop
family for generations. Except that a Mr Barton
Brightmore seemed to believe that it belonged more
properly among his own chattels. One day last week, the
ante-room at the Hall had been feloniously entered – no
significant damage done, but indicative scratches round
the lock. And the cloak-tree now stood provocatively in
the front window of Barton Brightmore's home in the
main thoroughfare.

Yet nothing had been done about it. The vicar passed
Barton Brightmore's window twenty times a day, yet
had not let it be known that he was aware of the theft.
The police had not been informed. No steps had been
taken to retrieve the piece. Members of the Gabbitas
Week Committee were coy if anyone ventured to bring
the subject up.

Kenworthy looked at his watch, carried his empty
glass across to the counter, and let himself out into the
rain. He stood for a moment to get his bearings and a
savage gust lashed his face. Barely fifty yards to go, and
he had to face the elements like some Conrad character
on a hell-raked quarter-deck. He could sense, rather
than see, the low cottages of grey stone withdrawn
beyond their flagged paths, the squat, dour windows, the
warm fastnesses within. Before the coming of the railway
(which had never ventured nearer than seven miles to
Spentlow) this had been no more than a neighbourly
huddle of hill-scratching farmers. Then the area had
suddenly found itself accessible to the jam-packed
industrial eruptions in every quarter of the compass, in
strategical command of the beautiful Dales. But now
aggressive October had banished day visitors, and the

letting cottages (mostly the property of one Allsop or another) were locked up and deserted.

Yet across the Green, in the corner occupied by the church, school and vicarage, great oblongs of light were spilling from the windows of the Hall. Voices carried across the squalls: tuneless teenagers, topping the pops, until suddenly a barrack-square bark – the vicar's voice – produced a silence that even at this distance sounded guilty. And the silence endured. Nothing now but the trees fighting back at the wind. An arm of diseased elm cracked suddenly and came crashing down among its fellows somewhere on the perimeter of the settlement.

Kenworthy became aware of footsteps obliquely behind him. Someone else was crossing the forecourt of the pub. He turned his other cheek and saw a black figure set in momentary relief by the light from the inn-sign – a pixie, so it seemed, in a storm-beaten mantle, with a tall pointed hood pulled up over her head. The figure walked past him, as if unaware that he was there; but that could not have been the case because a second later the head was suddenly turned back to look at him. The light from the swinging sign was now playing on her face, and he saw that it was that of a young woman: a beautiful young woman, startlingly beautiful in the classical fashion. Her eyebrows were ebony curves against a smooth sculpted forehead. She had a rare placidity of feature, and yet the eyes that were smiling at him were alive. They seemed to find some vague source of amusement in the foul, cold rain. It was a strange moment, as if she had been waiting for him, as if she had known he was going to be here. Such advantage did she take of the weird, wan light that she might even have rehearsed her stance.

'Good evening, Mr Kenworthy. It *is* Mr Kenworthy?'

She smiled then with her lips, too – a melting and familiar smile; but then he saw that the light had been playing haphazard tricks, on her and on him. She was no woman; she was a child. She had a sharpness of feature that belied the illusion of Hellenic serenity, the contour undeveloped. Her frame was slender and her shoulders narrow. She could not be more than fourteen or fifteen; and she was looking at him with a friendly, almost impudent amusement.

'You seem to know me,' he said.

'Well, you've only yourself to blame for that, haven't you? When a man of your reputation takes a letting in Spentlow, he must expect a build-up before he arrives.'

Fourteen or fifteen? She certainly did not lack confidence or fluency.

'Sorry I can't stop now,' she said. 'Not that either of us would want to, in this. In any case, I'm late for rehearsal, and we have a producer who takes a wizened view of such things. But I do want to talk to you, Mr Kenworthy – some time soon. See you!'

She was away into the dark middle distance. Kenworthy leaned into the wind and thrashed his way home. After supper he did not pick up his Trollope again; the television set that was part of their so-called amenities produced a snow-storm on every channel. He went over to the randomly stocked bookcase and came up with two slim volumes that kept him happy and quiet for the remainder of the evening.

One was a collection of illustrated fairy-stories, printed by a firm in Staffordshire and published privately in 1861 by the Reverend Wilbur Gabbitas. They seemed fairly insipid stuff, but might have had some bite if one knew the local references. The central character was a deviously benevolent Spentlow goblin called Hob. And a strange thing about him, as about all the other characters in the *Tales*, was that none of them had any feet. They were always shown standing in long grass, or behind low walls and bushes. Wilbur Gabbitas had come realistically to terms with his inability to draw boots and shoes.

They were wholesome anecdotes, reminiscent of Aesop. A common theme was revenge against mean dealing; village rascals showed through, like the tale of an elf who got his come-uppance after stealing his neighbour's exhibition carrots, and Gabbitas had given names to warring factions of his Little People: the Sopalls and the Glitter-Betters. So this was the idiom that Dunderdale was emboldened to update – Spentlow might well be an interesting place on publication day.

The other book was a society-published paper by a forgotten academic who attempted, by reference to archaeological finds elsewhere, to reconstruct the layout of a barrow on the outskirts of Spentlow. Hob's Kitchen was the vernacular name for the spot, and local lore had for centuries peopled it with the family and hangers-on of the prank-playing sprite who had inspired Wilbur Gabbitas. But this historian had no time for such frivolity. He was more interested in the ancient chieftain who had been buried there, in 1800 BC or thereabouts, with his knees up to his chin, and at his side the bronze beaker whose contents were to sustain him on his last journey. But that was before an eighteenth-century (AD) Allsop had carried away one of the three great cornerstones to make a doorstep for his farm.

Kenworthy sat with his head back and his eyes closed in seraphic speculation which he did not even seem to want to share with his wife.

CHAPTER II

The next morning they woke uselessly early to the syncopated rhapsody of a rust-riddled downpipe. Kenworthy stretched out towards the transistor, and Radio Derby forecast another filthy day, during the course of which Elspeth braved the downpour to do essential shopping, and was gone long enough to make several friends; long enough to get herself asked out to tea that afternoon. Kenworthy emerged from the world of the nineteenth-century novel to explore the woodshed and bring in an assortment of sodden kindling to dry round the base of the boiler.

He also received a visit from a lean and voluble creature who introduced herself as Mrs Scadbolt and informed him that she had been engaged as household help by every tenant of the cottage for the last ten years. She was a startling creature, with black hair tightly and elaborately piled on top of her head and a garish shade of rouge standing out like poster paint over her high cheekbones. When Kenworthy let it be known that nothing would bring Elspeth greater pleasure than to do her own chores, she lingered as if in the hope of a sudden change of his paternalistic mind. She also flooded him with a chronicle of the crimes of the village over the last three decades, not one of them worth more than a magistrate's fine. That evening, an hour before the time when he had yesterday gone out for his beer, Elspeth caught him looking furtively at his watch. She pushed him out into the damp, making him button his coat collar before she released him.

On their second morning it was still raining at breakfast time, but Kenworthy insisted on going out. Yesterday the newspaper boy had delivered the *Mirror*, and this morning nothing at all. Elspeth, turning the rashers in the pan, thought he was gone a long time. She raised a corner of the curtain and watched him let himself out of the telephone box on the Green. He came back brandishing another *Mirror* with mock hysteria.

Later, the rain did stop, though water continued to filter through the trees with all the descant effects of the original downpour – and the same power to drench. Kenworthy announced his intention of going for a walk, and Elspeth was not dissuasive, being equally anxious to get outside their four allegedly furnished walls. With a scarf tied over her head and a one-inch map in Kenworthy's pocket they skirted the standing water in the Spentlow street and exchanged greetings with unknown Brightmores and Allsops alike. On a worn corner of the Green the school bus was reversing, ready to take the older children to the secondary school some ten miles away. Kenworthy caught sight of the pixie, now in a navy blue uniform with a pudding hat. He tried to catch her eye, but she was too absorbed in comparing homework with another girl, their fluttering exercise books balanced on loaded satchels. She was unquestionably a child this morning, no hint of the illusion of two nights ago. She got out a ballpoint, and hopping on one leg to balance book and bag on her knee, wrote down some alteration.

Out of the village, past the Pack Horse, through a farmyard where the right of way was guaranteed by an *Ancient Monument* signpost; the slough round a gate was such that they had to wrap themselves round the post to get through it. Elspeth did not protest, though her expression was that of a woman exercising patience. Kenworthy led her along a dry-stone wall, through a stile into an ash plantation, following a footpath over smooth-worn limestone slabs. The trees continued to shed water on them.

'Only some thirty yards, and we'll be out in the open. Look: there's a square inch of blue in the sky.'

Seconds later he fell headlong, smearing his trench-coat with mud and narrowly missing a tumble of some eight or ten feet down a vertical crag. But he did himself no more damage than a grazed knee.

'Don't rub it in,' Elspeth said. 'It'll brush off when it's dry.'

He pulled something up with his hand. From tufts on either side of the narrow path long tough grasses had been knotted together, forming an inverted V that had snared his ankle.

'Some kid's trick, I shouldn't wonder. Sorry, Elspeth, I know there isn't much fun in this, but I'd like to see the place now we've come this far.'

She did not demur, and within five minutes they were out of the wood and standing in the corner of a field by two great stones that had once stood upright: obelisks of a man's girth and twice a man's height that had once supported a capstone now long unaccounted for.

'Apparently these had to be dragged here for miles. There are fossils in the stone, encrinites, the stems of primeval sea-lilies. They don't belong on this hillside.'

'I know. People told me that yesterday.'

'Doesn't it give you an eerie feeling to think that here, four thousand years ago, some white-bearded king – '

'No,' she said.

'It does lack atmosphere, I must say.'

Two slabs of stone, no more, no less; no trace to the unschooled eye of a burial mound. In the next field a plover was wasting energy on decoy tactics.

'They don't even think of it as prehistoric in the village,' she said. 'They call it Hob's Kitchen.'

'According to the book, that's Saxon vintage. Maybe the Saxons found squatters on the site. Odd, though, that the only weirdness comes from a fictitious yarn, not from original history.'

'I don't find that odd. All I feel is wet and cold and ready for coffee.'

'We'll go home. Ha-ha, home! I just wanted to see the spot.'

'And now you're a wiser, fuller and wetter man.'

But it was unlike her to deal in dudgeon for long.

'Actually, there's been a lot of local feeling about this barrow,' she said.

'Has there indeed?'

'Because some landowner a couple of hundred years

ago carted a stone off for building. And was told by the vicar of the day that there would be a curse on his descendants for evermore.'

'So much I have heard.'

'A preservation society tried to get an injunction not long since to make the present landlord put it back. But the case failed. The judge said that he could not undo the understandable economies of the eighteenth century. It was the farmer's field and the farmer's lump of rock to do what he liked with. In point of fact, the case was only brought to make mischief. There's a dominant family in Spentlow — the Allsops. They sprawl right across the social scale. Anything worthwhile that's ever been done here has been done by an Allsop. It's an Allsop who owns this field. And, of course, our cottage. I know that you like a touch of history in your crimes, Simon, but even you aren't going to find a tie-up between this year's peccadilloes and Neolithic man.'

He agreed with a sort of whimiscal courtesy.

'No. That would need a long shot. But this little set-up was more recent than Neolithic. Bronze Age, in fact. Well, early Bronze Age — the Beaker Folk.'

'The Beaker Folk?'

For some reason, the label seemed to offend her. There was an untypical moody silence about her as they began the walk home. The rain had started again, plumb vertical now, as a change from dead horizontal. Soon there was no sky to be seen at all, only a hanging mist. In the cottage the boiler had gone out. Elspeth put a pan of water on the cooker.

'I'll make you a coffee, but I'm going out. I've had an invitation, but I left it open in case we could have gone anywhere together. You're welcome to come, but you wouldn't like the people.'

She was noisy with the crockery, but said no more until she had reached the front door. Then she turned.

'You made a telephone call this morning.'

'To a duty clerk at the Yard. Message for Bill Clingo. Something he ought to know.'

'About the Beaker Folk?'

'They were before his time.'

She came back into the room.

'Simon, I don't want to seem irritable, but I don't like being treated like this. If you wanted to come here on a job, you had only to say so. If you wanted my company on a working trip, you know I'd have come like a shot. But I don't like deceit. It isn't like you, and it isn't necessary.'

'We are here to see the Dales. And when the weather clears, we shall see them. I assure you – '

'Don't try to maintain the act. Every man, woman and child knows you're here for the sake of the Beaker Folk.'

She left him, and he bent to rake clinker. Then, discarding the Trollope, he picked up *The Scarlet Letter*.

CHAPTER III

The woman who pounced on Kenworthy as he pushed open the door of the Hall that same evening must surely in her time have held office in every do-gooders' organization within her field of fire. Her hand cupped his elbow as she addressed him, four inches from his ear, in a voice that would have inspired thoughts of home in Deeside cattle.

'Ah! A man!'

It had happened because on leaving the cottage he had gone not straight to the pub, but towards the overspill of light from the windows across the Green. Beaming with benign curiosity, he put his nose round the door of the Hall and negotiated a group of gossiping adolescents, prominent among them the pixie hood. The girl did not appear to notice him. Entering the Hall was

rather like raising a flat stone from over an ants' nest. At
a trestle table women were sewing brass rings into the
hem of magenta curtains; others were working on costumes. A gang of boys managed by a man in a Fair Isle
pullover were painting canvas scenery. Another man
was dragging about a bank of footlights, whilst on a
ladder that reached up into the rafters someone else was
busy with floodlights and clamps. But the nodal point
was the stage, on which a miscellany of amateur actors,
large among them the vicar himself, were shouting at
each other across a set comprising yellow folding chairs
and one solitary baize-covered card-table. The producer
was haranguing his cast with a sheaf of duplicated typescript in his hand. It was the young man with the Red
Indian head-band, his costume now an emerald green
caftan, constricted in the middle by what looked like a
genuine Franciscan girdle.

'Ah! A man!'

She was a short woman, barrel-like and hooped into
corsets. About her neck on a beaded chain hung a pair of
spectacles with a flyaway superstructure that looked like
a designer's draft for a rood-screen: obviously a woman
who did not leave the impact of her accessories to
chance. If her teeth, chins and bosom could not hold an
unruly meeting bemused, she must have known that any
village heckler would think twice before challenging the
malachite earrings that hung down like toy policemen's
truncheons.

'Just what we want. And the Superintendent himself,
if I am not mistaken.'

She shepherded him, elbow still cupped, to the edge of
the stage.

'For some reason, Colonel Noakes has let us down this
evening. Not like him at all. Always at the edge of the
square, five minutes before time for parade: we've heard
him say it a thousand times. Now, do be a good man and
read his part for us. Gwen's been doing her best, but it

isn't the same in a woman's voice, and I'm sure it puts everyone off.'

Someone thrust a script into Kenworthy's hand. Someone else pointed halfway down the page with a hasty forefinger. The producer issued instructions in tones of saintly patience.

'We'll go back to the beginning of the scene between the two priests.'

'*Ah, my dear Gabbitas. Come in, come in, come in!*'

Daniel Dunderdale might have been drilling recruits, but he dropped his voice to add, 'You're supposed to be off-stage, Kenworthy. You come in left centre. *Ah, my dear Gabbitas, come in, come in, come in!*'

Kenworthy came in and stood, looking lost mid-stage.

'Try to follow the stage directions,' the producer said. 'And don't forget to trip up as you come in.'

'Does it matter all that much whether I trip up or not? I'm only doing this until Colonel Noakes arrives, which please God may be any minute now.'

'The more you can get right, the more helpful it will be to the others. Shall we take your entrance again?'

Kenworthy went clumsily through the required motion.

'That's better. Try to remember that Wilbur Gabbitas was a very clumsy man until Gertrude Allsop took him in hand. Always putting his thumb in his tea, and dropping bits of cake into his hat. All of which we exaggerate for the sake of a Spentlow audience.'

This was followed by a short silence until everyone in the room reminded Kenworthy that the next line was his.

'*Ah, my dear Vicar. Mrs Burgess gave me your message. You wanted to see me?*'

'*Ah, yes, dear Gabbitas. I'll ring for tea.*'

Dunderdale moved to the chalk-line of a fireplace and tugged an imaginary cord.

'*Do please take your seat on that sofa.* That's the two chairs together. Cross your legs and stick your foot out. The housekeeper's got to fall over it. *Do please take a seat on that sofa.* Splendid. *What I have to say to you had better wait until Mrs Brightmore has been in with the tea things.*'

'*I do hope that I have not given any kind of offence, Vicar. A fine afternoon for the time of the year, is it not?*'

'*And a fine night last night also, did you not think? I shall be asking you presently what you thought you were about last night, Gabbitas.*'

'*Ah!*'

'*You may well say "Ah!"*''

This was the moment chosen by the electrician to lift his clattering batten on to the stage.

'Don't mind us,' the producer said.

'You told me to test the filter mix.'

'All right, then. You others carry on as if nothing were happening.'

Kenworthy's script said *Gabbitas looks concerned.* He opened his eyes wide and set his face in the last throes of terror. Someone in the body of the Hall tittered. The electrician went to the far end of a long snake of cable and reached up to a master-switch. There were simultaneous blue flashes in several parts of the room, and then immediate darkness. Someone on stage struck a match, someone else flicked a cigarette lighter. It was minutes before illumination was restored, and that from only one dingy bulb.

'You'd better take a good look at that batten, George. Let's carry on with Mrs Brightmore.'

The housekeeper was played by the woman who had seized Kenworthy at the door. He failed comically to trip her up as she came in and she offered Dunderdale a tray in a voice that would have dispersed the Parisians from their barricades. Stretching out his foot, Kenworthy managed to kick her on the knee-cap as she went out.

'We'll keep that in,' the producer said.

'Indeed we will not,' she told him sonorously.

And then George unbent himself from the batten, holding up something that no one could see.

'Look at this!'

This was something with which he was not prepared to part, except into the hands of the vicar. It was an old sixpenny piece that had been wedged under one of the bulbs.

'If we were still on that length of copper wire that the caretaker had in as a main fuse, the whole Hall could have gone up in flames.'

As it was, there was a strong smell of scorched rubber.

'Sheer vandalism,' Dunderdale said.

They played out the rest of the scene. It was a dialogue in which Dunderdale, in the role of his own predecessor, was upbraiding his curate for clandestine comings and goings in the precincts of Dogtooth Farm by moonlight. The Allsop of the day, it seemed, had had a daughter who was not considered fit company for a clerk in Holy Orders.

'*My dear Gabbitas* – '

'*My dear Vicar* – '

'*No. Hear me out, dear Gabbitas. I promise you that when I have finished, you shall have your say. I have your interests as close to my heart as I have those of the Mother Church. But we must look to our reputations, Gabbitas. We must be as Caesar's wife.*'

'*All I did was go over to the farm to give her a copy of* The Christian Year *in exchange for an oven-bottom loaf.*'

'*It is immaterial what transaction you considered economically sound. Even when it concerns John Keble and our daily bread. Moreover, the exchange, if my informant is to be believed, seems to have taken an unconscionable time.*'

'*I went at some length into the Tractarian Movement.*'

'Wait for the laugh,' the producer said.

'*You are asking me to believe, young sir, that in the midnight moonlit shadows of Reuben Allsop's shippon, you talked for an hour and a half to his daughter Gertrude about the Tractarian Movement?*'

The scene went on for another five or six minutes and the Gabbitas characterization began to emerge. Wilbur Gabbitas, a shy, newly-ordained curate, had come to Spentlow in the middle of the century. He had been accident-prone, naive, on no sort of wavelength to communicate either with his vicar or with any stratum of the parish. He was amiable, poor, and pathetically eager for success – which he came within no visible distance of achieving. And then, visiting about the bleak hills in his district he crossed paths with Gertrude Allsop. On the subject of Gertrude, Dunderdale had pulled out all the stops. He bellowed his lines at Kenworthy, who sat with his script on his knees, affecting meek astonishment.

'*Gertrude Allsop? Do you know what she is? She is a heathen, sir. She is a servitor of false gods, a worshipper of hideous idols, a fetishist of corrupt symbols. She is a betrayer of men and an abomination unto all we hold sacred. She will have your heart, sir, and your bowels at the same time. She will stab the one while she ties knots in the other. She will entice you by lunar magic into the orbit of the Anathema Stone, and there she will have her will of you. And her will of you is your destruction. The wages of dalliance in that quarter, sir, are annihilation. Make no mistake of it.*'

Kenworthy read humbly from his script.

'*I would have you know, sir, that you are speaking of the woman I –* '

'*In faith, sir, and are you so steeped in your circulating library trash that the best you can think of is – ?*'

'*I was about to say, sir, that you are speaking of the woman to whom I was talking last night about the Tractarian Movement.*'

In the next page and a half the exposition was more specific about Gertrude. Her father, Reuben, great-grandfather of Jesse, the present farmer, had not been a trusted man about the village. Dark-visaged, moody, humourless, he had been left a widower when his daughter was only eight years old. A man who kept his own counsel – and dark counsel indeed – he rebuffed any attempt to help him with the management of the child – aggressively, if the charity happened to be offered by a woman. He withdrew from companionship, abjured the church of his forbears. He would not pass under the lych-gate again, he vowed, until he was carried through it in the wake of his Arabella. And the Reverend Carrow, when he ventured to call with the conditions of redemption, left the farm with a sample of his suiting in the jaws of a bull-mastiff.

Reuben Allsop, however, was not a static man. He was a diligent farmer, so impervious to the disasters that regularly struck his neighbours that he gained a reputation for alliance with uncouth forces. Gales did not wreck his roofs, blight shrugged away from his potatoes, footrot spared his sheep, and aphids scorned his beans. He began quietly to make money, and being indifferent to what money might buy, went on quietly to put that money to work. He invested in the catastrophes that afflicted others, letting himself be persuaded with apparent reluctance into loans and mortgages, but evincing no sloth when interest was due and unforthcoming. He was never hesitant about foreclosure. Strips and parcels about the Spentlow hills came into his possession, and it became known that once he had begun to covet the spaces between his holdings he had a habit of cornering the deeds sooner or later. Thus was acquired the empire that continued to support the Allsops in the late twentieth century: no Promised Land, agriculturally considered, but relatively speaking an empire, none the less.

'You speak of him as a poor man, sir, but time will tell what milk and honey the third and fourth generations will find in the aftermath of Reuben Allsop.'

So this was the nurturing of Gertrude Allsop, a long way from other children, barely catching sight of a man and rigorously shielded from female influences. Certain callers at the farm, having encountered her, had been heard to say that they would rather take their chance with the bull-mastiff. She was raven-haired, bare-footed, had cow-dung caked down the calves of her legs, and eyes that flashed an arrogant challenge. By the age of nine she was doing the milking and could wring a chicken's neck; at ten she was said to have finished off with her own hands a fox caught in a gin-trap; at thirteen she could have laid a dry-stone wall alongside a champion; and at sixteen she bit a reconnoitring Brightmore so viciously in the hand that he had to have the wound cauterized. In twentieth-century jargon she might have been called autistic, but this would have been a misjudgement; it was possible to communicate with her. But she chose for herself, from some poisoned well of intuition, those to whom she cared to be accessible, and they were few.

And then Wilbur Gabbitas, ill-advised as ever to the point of a positive talent, had called at Dogtooth on a self-inspired quest for souls to care for. Perhaps he had visions of tea and Genoa cake in a heavily brocaded farmhouse drawing-room. Instead he was confronted by an unanswered door which he had had to cross a muck-strewn yard to reach, windows curtained by muslin in the last discernible shade of grey, a cracked chimneypot lying across an upturned trough. And in a corner, by a water butt, a girl was watching him. He did not see her at first. It was as if she had materialized at his second glance, come alive from the background of flaking whitewash, tottering downpipes and broken implements. Perhaps it was because she had been standing so deathly still, in the frozen act of filling a ladle at a barrel. She looked at him with eyes that he could not interpret – dark and defensively challenging. The thought was slow to strike him that she was the daughter of the house.

What Gertrude saw was a handsome young man with a beard, athletic limbs and a friendly smile, that was not afraid of her. He asked her if there was anyone at home and she made no sign of having heard him. Her stance was statuesque, the ladle unmoved in her hand. But when he began to cross diagonally back towards the gate, she came a couple of steps nearer to him.

'What do you want?'

In his ears her voice had a sweetness that was quite out of keeping with her rags. She was wearing the shortest dress that he had ever seen on a woman outside a classical painting, and because she was either brazen or innocent, there was more of her to be seen than he had ever seen of a woman's body before. He did not look directly at her for long.

'And this, Master Gabbitas, is the woman to whom you have parted with your Christian Year? *What use can she have for the printed page?'*

'She could surprise you, sir. She reads clearly and with confidence and writes in a tolerably formed hand. Her father has not neglected the entire gamut of his obligations.'

'You are playing with fire, Wilbur Gabbitas – with fire and vitriol and the fiends of hell and beyond. Of hell and beyond, Mr Gabbitas!'

Curtain.

'Thank you, Mr Kenworthy. That was first-rate. What a pity you're not playing the part! Check! Don't let the Colonel know I said that, or maybe you will be.'

Kenworthy was taken over and introduced to the producer, John Horrocks, who was a teacher of English at a secondary school somewhere between Ashbourne and Derby.

'Shall we go on now with the scene between Gertrude and Wilbur?'

Kenworthy looked at his watch.

'I'm afraid I shall have to wish you goodnight now. But if ever you're pushed for a stand-in, don't hesitate –'

'But Mr Kenworthy, I'd been hoping you'd – '

Then a young player came up and approached the platform with clear anticipation of stardom. It was the youngster with the pixie cloak, now discarded to reveal a short-skirted green dress. Every other girl in the room was in jeans. Was the distinction due to parental control, or to this one's natural sense of apartness from the crowd? Her black hair looked as if it had been washed for the occasion, and was done in a professional style older than her years, which to some extent compensated for the immaturity of her features. And yet at certain angles she might still have been taken for an older girl. She came down the central aisle with quick steps, bouncing almost, conscious beyond doubt that she was something special.

At the same time Kenworthy noticed that Elspeth was also unaccountably in the room. She must have slipped in while he was concentrating on his script, and seemed happily at home amongst the sewing women. So she had got herself drawn in? He raised his hand to give her some sort of message. But words were not necessary.

'No need to worry, Simon. It's only ham salad. Nothing to spoil. I wouldn't miss this for a ransom.'

Concerted laughter from the women. John Horrocks was issuing directions to his stage hands.

'Two folding chairs for the bales of straw. Put that weighing machine at the back on the right. That can be the pump.'

'The welfare people will go off their heads,' some woman said, 'if they find he's been at their scales.'

'The scene is the yard at Dogtooth, Mr Kenworthy. You're sitting on the straw. Behind you's the barn with the infamous doorstep. There are cowpats all round you, and you eye them fastidiously from time to time. There's very little else for you to do except sit there – that's right, left-hand corner – and let Davina do her stuff. You don't co-operate. Just let her take you by storm. But if you can suggest to the audience that you're beginning to get more pleasure out of it than you expected, then that's all to the good. Give her a shy little pat from time to time.'

Already Davina was on one knee in front of him, looking up into his eyes with her left hand on his shoulder. He could smell the cleanness of her hair, the precocity of her perfume, look down at the firm development of breasts barely past puberty.

'Good evening, Mr Kenworthy.'

'Good evening.'

'Who'd have thought we'd be meeting under these conditions'.

And 'Action!' shouted John Horrocks, whereupon she leaped upon Kenworthy, smothered him with her arms and budding bosom, pressed her lips on his so that his nose was as twisted as that of an adolescent in a first encounter. A whoop of delight went up from the women.

'Cut!' said the producer. 'Cut, cut, cut, cut, cut! Very convincing, very convincing indeed. And God knows what state your make-up's in by now. Don't think I begrudge you your pleasures, Davina, but now that you've said hullo to him, do you think we could start again and play it as a stage kiss? There's no need for your lips to touch. You've got your back to the audience, and you're masking Mr Kenworthy. And just bear in mind that it's Colonel Noakes you'll be kissing on the night.'

'More's the pity,' she whispered to Kenworthy. 'OK, John.'

'All right, then. Quiet, everybody! Last few bars of interval music. Pum-te, pum-te, pum-te, pum. Curtain up. Action!'

She came at him again, this time more soberly, yet with her face only an inch or two away from his, looking soulfully up into his eyes. He looked as if he wished himself many miles away, but she had not even left him marginal room to turn his head. And his position was made all the more awkward because he had to wriggle his arm away from her so that he could read his script over her shoulder. At last she pushed herself away from him and pinned him down by his shoulders at arm's length.

'*Oh, Wilbur –* '

'*Actually, I had hoped that we might continue our discussion of Pusey's views on everlasting punishment. I wonder if you have had time to read the copy I gave you of his paper to the Hebdomadal Council*'?

She got up and took a few steps away from him. The release enabled him to turn a page. He blew out his cheeks in relief. The audience was delighted.

She plucked a small book, improbably, from somewhere under her neck-line. It was the second part of Hall and Knight's *Algebra*.

'*No. But there are some lines that have been ringing in my head from that other book you gave me:*

Thou who hast given me eyes to see
And love this sight so fair,
Give me a heart to find out thee
And read thee everywhere.'

'*Excellently rendered,*' Kenworthy read, '*but yours is not, I fear, the interpretation favoured at Oriel.*'

She came back to him, laid down the book on the notional straw, stroked it fondly and knelt down in front of him on the opposite side from before. Kenworthy gingerly patted the top of her head and awkwardly shifted his knees to accommodate her. Laughter, in which Elspeth's was prominent. Davina put up her hand under his jacket and found a sensitive area of his ribs.

'This scene really warms up in a minute,' she said.

CHAPTER IV

'Simon – it's time I took you home.'

Elspeth's voice was raised for the sake of the female gallery. Her eyes were filmed over with tears of hilarity. She held his arm tightly as he piloted her across the Green. The rain had rung the changes and degenerated into a penetrating drizzle.

'I didn't know you had it in you, Simon. You've missed your vocation.'

'All I had to do was sit still and behave normally. The girl's a natural.'

'She's good. But I'm surprised that the vicar's letting her go through with it. The part's evidently going to her head.'

'Well, I think the village is lucky to have her.'

'You think so? Or is she just good at being herself? Don't think I mind – but did she have to throw herself at you quite as she did? Amateur dramatics can be dangerous. Especially when somebody young and impressionable happens to shine in the wrong kind of part.'

'There was a German actor before the war who ended up thinking he really was Frederick the Great.'

'That's just what I mean. And this is the wrong time in Davina Stott's life for her to be making a hit as a budding nympho or an Emily Brontë primitive.'

'She seems highly intelligent to me. I dare say she'll salvage her sense of proportion.'

'I hope you're right. But she does come from a broken home. And, thanks to the asinine law, is in the custody of the wrong parent.'

'Indeed?'

'The father was weak-willed and gallant. The mother's an alcoholic.'

'Is she now? Well, the girl looks well-turned-out, well-nourished, full of self-assurance. If ever a girl knew where she wanted to go – '

'And that's not on a bale of straw with an Oxford Movement curate. She may even aim higher than a Detective-Superintendent.'

He did not reply at once. 'You've evidently thrown in your lot with an extremely well-informed sewing circle,' he said at last.

She looked at him for a second with sidelong suspicion.

'You can't hide anything in a village,' she said.

'Or rely on a fair deal from public opinion, either.'

By now they were at their door. She had the only key and let them into the grey interior. They took off their coats and shook them over the doorstep. It was hard to tell whether the boiler was in or out. Kenworthy burned and soiled his fingers.

'I'm sorry it's a cold supper, Simon. I'll warm up a tin of soup, if you like.'

'I would like, please.'

He laid the table and they sat facing each other.

'Simon, I'm sorry about this morning; I don't want to shelter behind my "Time of Life". I suppose little things do loom large sometimes. But I'd be telling less than the truth if I didn't say it still rankles.'

He waited.

'Next time you want cover for a provincial ploy, take me into your confidence. I'll come with you, if you'll let me. But don't pretend we're on holiday. And don't let them take it out of you at holiday time. They have their pound of flesh, most weeks.'

'We *are* on holiday.'

'Don't, oh don't try to keep that up. If you do, I can't answer for what might happen to me.'

He was silent, looking steadily at her.

'More soup?'

'If there is any, please.'

She went to the cooker, served him, ran cold water into the pan, came back and sat opposite him.

'Having said that, may I add that I am ready to co-operate in any way, holiday or chore?'

'I'm glad to hear it.'

'I think I may claim to have found out more about the Beaker Folk than you have unearthed since we arrived here.'

'Some of your new friends must be archaeologists.'

'Maintain your fiction if it amuses you.'

'As far as I am concerned, the Beaker Folk were a migrant civilization who appeared in these hills in about 1800 BC in the wake of the Neolithic tribes. They were precursors of the Bronze Age and took their name from the receptacles with which they believed it necessary to equip the recently deceased.'

'As far as Spentlow is concerned, the Beaker Folk are the members of a commune that has squatted in the squalor of Spentlow Grange since last Easter. They include the colourfully-dressed gentleman who is producing the play and his common-law wife.'

'Christine.'

'You know her?'

'I've seen her. In the pub.'

'Which pub?'

'The Recruiting Sergeant. The couple seemed to command a measure of respect, which surprised me.'

'It doesn't surprise me. That's the Brightmore pub.'

She mixed the salad. The hard-boiled eggs had the rich orange yolks produced by hens that foraged in rickyards.

'The things you have dug out in Spentlow,' he said.

'And about the Beaker Folk.'

'Go on.'

'They are anarchists, promiscuous, drug-addicts.'

'What drugs?'

'I don't know: drugs. They play rock music late into the night, so loud you can hear them at the bottom of the village. They danced naked one night at Hob's Kitchen.'

'Some of these hippies are hardier than you'd think.'

'They live on Social Security – all except this man Horrocks, who teaches. They spend hardly anything in the village, and that only piecemeal – a tin of this and a packet of frozen that. They have no order for milk and appear to live on black instant coffee. That is why the village has christened them the Beaker Folk. The first thing they did when they arrived was to clear the village shop's stock of those blue souvenir mugs with *Spentlow* on the side, about their only possessions, except for bedrolls and guitars. People can see those beakers standing on the window-sills, always there; never washed up. Pretty well the only furniture, except for Horrocks's books and stereogram. They haven't curtained the windows, and their lights are burning half the night. Anyone can see all that goes on.'

'If my memory of the map serves me correctly, it would be a stiff climb, and an otherwise fruitless one, just to put oneself in a position to be shocked. Any children?'

'Hordes of them. And not living in families. Everybody seems to be everybody else's property – in more ways than one.'

'And everybody else's responsibility, too?'

'Don't be exasperating, Simon. You know you've no room for such goings-on.'

'I've come across such set-ups before. Utterly misguided. I'd go as far as to say utterly revolting. But not necessarily criminal. You can't prosecute them for trying something different. I'll bet there's as much wife-swapping in the Pack Horse at week-ends as there is at the Grange. So what's the charge going to be? Corrupting the youth of the neighbourhood? Like Socrates?'

'The village children *are* scared stiff of them. Some of the women have formed their own vigilante committee – they meet even the older ones from school.'

'Don't the Beaker children go to school?'

'They run their own free school. The education committee have an attendance order in the pipeline. And one child is certainly in danger; your Davina Stott has been spending a lot of time up at the Grange.'

'She's not my Davina Stott. I just peeped in through the door of the Hall in time to be thrown into her arms. And she's evidently a bright child with an enquiring mind. She wants to know what's going on.'

'I do wish you'd take this seriously.'

'You really think that a squalid experiment in drop-out living is worth an assignment for a DS in another force's territory?'

'You were quick to seize upon the Beaker Folk this morning, when we were at the Anathema Stones.'

'Those aren't the Anathema Stones. There's only one Anathema Stone – the one that the eighteenth-century farmer carted away, and which the vicar of the day told him would be anathema to him and his dependants, because even pagans are entitled to their rest. I know I did mention the Beaker Folk. They are the ones who put up the stones in the first place. And I'm sorry, Elspeth, you haven't established the faintest pointer to any serious law-breaking.'

'But this commonplace drop-out stuff – the weird costumes, the aggressive music, the moral depravity – it would make an excellent camouflage. It's probably better cover these days than a respectable exterior.'

'Elspeth, you fascinate me. Better cover for what, do you think?'

'You ought to know better than I do. Planning some crime on a big scale? Drug-running? Sabotage? Terrorism? Simon – if it's an official secret, don't of course tell me. But I'm dying to know. It was the Yard you rang this morning, wasn't it?'

'So much I can't deny.'

'And that's all you're telling me?'

'No. As a matter of fact, I rang because I'd heard a name mentioned. In canteen talk. A man that Bill Clingo is anxious to chat with. I honestly don't know why.'

'Simon – I can tell you what that name was.'

'Do, then.'

'Kevin O'Shea?'

'You're a clever girl, Elspeth. And you have some clever friends. This man O'Shea – a big, red-headed

Irishman, do they say?'

'That's right. But he's no longer here. He disappeared some weeks ago, and it had something to do with the Stott girl. Nobody knows exactly what. But he must have written for some of his things, because a parcel was sent to him. Shirts and things, the woman in the post office says, from the feel of it; and sent to Nuneaton, but she didn't make a note of the address.'

'Well done! Bill will be delighted to know. I'd just happened to hear him mention the chap, and say he wanted to interview him very badly indeed. I'll slip out and ring him at home. And that is the beginning and end of my involvement.'

He let himself out to the call-box. The drizzle was persisting. Over at the Hall he could see that the lights were only now being switched off. Bill Clingo was out, so he passed the Nuneaton tip to Bill's wife. And then, as he stepped out of the kiosk, a waiting figure bore down on him out of the shadows. He found himself entangled in a fold of the vicar's cloak.

'Mr Kenworthy – may I come indoors with you? It's too wet to talk out here, and I need your help urgently.'

'But of course. You couldn't have chosen a better time. Coffee's on the trivet.'

Dunderdale looked round the shabby decoration. 'And what sort of rent has Jesse Allsop dared to ask you for this?'

Kenworthy told him.

'He has a nerve.'

Elspeth made a fuss of the vicar. They put his cloak on a clothes-horse near to the boiler. He settled himself in one of the fireside chairs, huge limbs monopolizing the hearth-rug, compelling eyes burning over the Assyrian beard.

'I'll come to the point. I've just been down to see the Colonel. I thought I'd better, since it's so unlike him to default from parade. And a good job I did, or he'd have

lain where I found him for the rest of the night. Took a
nasty fall, not fifty yards from his cottage. Fractured a
femur for certain, and I don't feel too sanguine about his
pelvis. Taking that Labrador of his for a walk, which he
does in all weathers. He must have slipped on a stretch of
greasy stone and come down heavily. I rang for an
ambulance and they've carted him off. I don't suppose
we shall get a report before morning.'

'Nasty.'

'Very nasty indeed.'

'It was sporting of him to have taken on the Gabbitas
part.'

'Especially since not one of us could pretend that he
was anything but wooden in the part. Just this side of
hopeless – that's how he put it himself. But the men of
this village! They'll help the play in any way they can –
short of acting. That's what I'm coming to. You're here
for three weeks?'

A silence fell on the diminutive room. The ticking of
the mantelclock asserted itself. A piece of wood splut-
tered in the boiler. Steam was beginning to rise from the
vicar's cloak.

'We all thought you were sensational at rehearsal
tonight.'

'Stage terror. It seems that that was all that was
needed for the scene. I don't even look the part. I'm long
past a newly-fledged curate's years.'

'You're a good-looking man, Kenworthy. A touch or
two of fresh complexion out of a pot – the odd wrinkle
shaded out – '

'Really, I'm sorry,' Kenworthy said.

'Without your help, it's hard to see how the show can
go on.'

'It's hardly fair to throw that responsibility on to me,
Mr Dunderdale.'

Kenworthy looked at Elspeth, but she was taking care
not to influence him.

'I don't know whether you've seen the thirty-day fore-cast,' Dunderdale said. 'It's pretty dismal.'

'They've been known to be wrong.'

The cloak was beginning to give off an aroma. Out-side, a cat knocked over an empty bucket.

'I'll make a bargain with you, Vicar.'

'Anything within reason.'

'Straight answers to three straight questions. No limit to the number of supplementaries.'

'I'll do my best.'

Kenworthy got up and moved about the room. But Dunderdale was a difficult man to dominate by a mere stance.

'Main question one: was this injury to Colonel Noakes an accident?'

'Difficult to tell, under cover of darkness.'

'But you examined the terrain with that in mind? That's a supplementary, by the way.'

'I did.'

'And it would not have surprised you to find that he had been the victim of a trap?'

'I fear not.'

'Further supplementary: what other accidents have there been?'

'The blowing of the footlights fuse tonight. Thefts of players' scripts – or, rather, unaccountable losses of same. I've had to have a whole new set run off.'

'And?'

'Pin-pricks almost too insubstantial to be worth men-tioning: loss of stage properties; false messages passed, to keep players away from rehearsal; loss of the Hall key at a crucial moment.'

There was lamentably little space for Kenworthy to perambulate. He leaned with one elbow on the mantel-piece. There was no scope to do that with dignity, either.

'Main question two, then. In your list of mishaps, why didn't you mention the theft of an antique cloak-tree from the Hall?'

'Because that is a separate issue. There is no doubt
who is the culprit, and I shall deal with that situation
dramatically.'

'And legally?'

'Within the law.'

'You have not reported the theft?'

'I do not regard it as a theft. Rather as a gesture.'

'And you had not thought of consulting the police
about any of your suspicions?'

'They have all been too flimsy.' Dunderdale laughed;
not with his usual heartiness; a touch of embarrassment.

'And I must confess that the thought had occurred to
me that with our own favourite policeman an interested
party – '

'Not on,' Kenworthy said. 'Just not on. Anything off-
square is the responsibility of the county force.'

'If you say so, Mr Kenworthy.'

'Third and final main question, then: there are people
in Spentlow who would sleep easier if *The Anathema Stone*
were not going to be staged?'

'No one is afraid of the play.'

'But they are of your book?'

'Some people are.'

'And you can name those who have most to fear?'

'That is difficult, Mr Kenworthy.'

'But not so difficult that you propose to be evasive?'

A phenomenally big man, there was artificiality in
Dunderdale's character, theatricality at more than one
level of consciousness. Perhaps he was constantly
striving to compensate for the ingredients of caricature
in his appearance. But his next answer sounded as if it
were stripped of pretence.

'The difficulty lies not in what is in the book, but in
what people think might be. Some people are afraid who
have no need to be.'

'You are wielding a formidable weapon, Vicar. But

you can name your main enemies.'

And Dunderdale suddenly resigned, like a consummate chess-player, his position of apparent superiority.

'There are some who might see red: Jesse Allsop, Barton Brightmore – but it is not fair to throw suspicion on them. There are others, fringe characters, whom I do not greatly fear, but who might nevertheless have an exaggerated notion of what they stand to lose.'

'I would like to see an advance copy of *Hob*, Mr Dunderdale.'

'You shall have it first thing in the morning.'

'And I have one further question.'

'You are certainly making the most of your supplementaries.'

'I hope this is the last. Do you in any way associate the hostility to Gabbitas Week with the society that is known locally as the Beaker Folk?'

'Emphatically not.'

'Good. Then I will play Wilbur Gabbitas for you. Though I heartily regret the casual curiosity that brought me within lethal distance of your Hall.'

Dunderdale handed him the script, which he had been nursing ever since he came in. Elspeth said that she was glad that Simon had made the decision. He would make local history in the part.

He sat for an hour and read the play through. Wilbur Gabbitas was on stage almost throughout, and there were one or two speeches of daunting length – and syntax. Once when he looked up he saw that Elspeth was sitting at the table with a writing pad from which she had already torn off several pages. He looked at her enquiringly.

'Just something I'm doing for the Women's Institute. Their next week's speaker has let them down, so I'm talking to them about what it's like to be the wife of a London detective.'

'Let me know if you need any help.'

'It's a subject you know very little about.'

'Come here.'

'Simon – I'm busy.'

It was a shabby little room. Seven or eight years ago, the wallpaper had come with the trade name Sunshine Yellow. Light was from a single forty-watt bulb, shaded under cracked imitation parchment.

'This sofa is two bales of straw. The boiler can be the pump. The cooker can be an old Soyer stove used for boiling pig-swill. Mind how you tread amongst the cow pats. I need a lot more practice in this scene. Now – can you remember how she knelt?'

'Only a stage kiss,' she said. 'I'm not having you mess up my make-up, dear Wilbur.'

CHAPTER V

A fuller picture of Wilbur Gabbitas emerged from the play. It was pure theatre, village theatre at that, but Dunderdale had boldly established his central character; Wilbur Gabbitas had been a diffident young man, yet intense, on fire within. He soon gave up hope of making much headway with Pennine farmers. But then he met Gertrude Allsop, the spitfire hill spirit, the alleged heathen. And she for her part harboured secret envies of that world of society that she glimpsed from the nightmare precincts belonging to her bereaved and demented father. The Reverend Aloysius Carrow expostulated in vain with the young man.

Gabbitas obstinately announced their intention of marrying; Dunderdale had written a scene of pleading and reasoning, had made heavy weather of the pharisaical disciplinarians of the diocese. The couple honeymooned in Scarborough. (The story told in the Recruiting Sergeant was that Gertrude had three times thrown him out of the bedroom window into the soft earth of a flower-bed below, before he had consented to get under the sheets and accept her instruction in the facts of life.)

When the Gabbitases returned to Spentlow their lives changed. Dunderdale staged Gertrude dressed and coiffured for a social round in which she did not know what a comic figure she was cutting; Wilbur returned to his pastoral duties with fresh confidence. He began to be noted for his knowledge of the secrets of those whom he visited; it was clear that Gertrude was passing on much that she had learned from the years that the locusts had eaten; but she also began to coach her husband in the pagan lore of the region. Much of it superstitious nonsense, it was all rooted somehow, somewhere, in things so old that their reality had been forgotten. Then, one morning, during a visit to the school, in search of an analogy to clear up some point, he told the children a story about the antics of the sprite who was supposed to have inhabited Hob's Kitchen.

Its success was explosive. On his next visit he was compelled to repeat the tale (the point to be illustrated now thoroughly forgotten), and for his third visit he had a new *Hob* story ready. *Hob* tales, tailored to the issue of the moment, began to feature in the Sunday schoolroom, too. Hob's clans re-enacted the Good Samaritan – a wounded Glitter-Better tended by a Sopall – the time had to come when a *Hob* tale supplemented the scriptures in the pulpit of St Giles.

The Reverend Carrow was uneasy. This was more than mere secularization of holy writ. Unable to ignore the gluttony of the Spentlow congregation for *Hob* stories, he made his curate ration them to one a month. They filled the pews. A visiting stranger saw commercial possibilities and eased the way to the publication of the book, with the pictures of little men whose ankles were all lost in grass.

The end, though, was pathos: an evening's laughter, ending with wet hankies. Acceptable social comedy had a stinging tail of stark tragedy. And in a Christian play, by a Christian priest, with intended Christian impact, there were strong undertones of more ancient, less reputable, nonetheless inescapable forces: Hob's Kitchen and the Anathema Stone.

The next morning Kenworthy woke at the upright minute-hand of six. He let himself out of the cottage without disturbing Elspeth. It was no longer raining, but the world was still damp: finger-ends reaching out from unkempt hedges, and the lane-breadth strands of Herculean spiders. The meanest tinge of ashen light in the sky behind the eastern trees presaged another grey day. He crossed to a far corner of the Green from which he could hear, and shortly hoped to see, the gate of the vicarage. He had not been there more than two or three minutes when the latch clicked and the cloak came forth, a form rather than a man, and struck out towards where he was waiting. They had made no arrangement to meet, but neither man showed surprise at the encounter.

'You know where Sidi Barrani is?'

'No. But it doesn't surprise me that that's what he calls it.'

Dunderdale guided him into a narrow lane with a concealed entrance and a cul-de-sac sign. The surface seemed to be of buried boulders, chosen mainly because they were handy when the road was made. They passed a modern bungalow with its curtains drawn in sleep ('The Stotts, mother and daughter'), two or three cottages at irregular intervals, the yard frontage of a mud-stranded farm ('Brightmore territory'), and after a desert of rough fields, populated by uneasy beef cattle and deserted summer caravans, came into sight of a low limestone house with a wicket gate and smokeless chimney.

'Noakes's paddock?'

'His pet name for it is B Echelon.'

In the window, a sorry-looking creeper in a brass pot bore an unmilitary look.

'The Colonel has four dog-walks. Patrols, he calls them. He always lets the dog choose – or appear to. Last night it was this way – '

'This way' was a continuation of the lane, a lane now frankly exhausted of ambition. It was so narrow that they could scarcely walk abreast, and they descended a series of steps made of limestone slabs, worn smooth by feet and greasy with damp lichen.

'Spentlow calls this the Roman Paving. A handy label for anything earlier than the seventeenth century.'

They found what they were looking for: the stone on which Noakes had slipped. He had slipped because the slab was loose and mobile on a fulcrum of earth, like a see-saw. There was not a great deal of play, but enough to up-end a man in a wet twilight. And it was in this state because clay and loose stones at its lower end had been scooped out from under it. Kenworthy picked up several such bits and pieces.

'I suppose your part of the bargain now calls for your county colleagues?' Dunderdale asked.

'Maybe not quite yet. They might think this evidence scanty – might even suggest that this rubble has been washed adrift by the weather we've been having. You said that the Colonel had four routine patrols: does one of them take him along the top of the plantation that leads to Hob's Kitchen?'

'Occasionally.'

'I fell there yesterday. Caught my foot in deliberately knotted grass. But who's to say that's not some boy's prank? That leaves two other walks?'

'One's through the heart of the village. It could hardly be booby-trapped. The other's to Bootherstone's – that's a quarry on the far side of the church.'

'Will you, or shall I? Or shall we both?'

'I have to be at the County Crematorium at half past ten. And if we're seen going together, someone will know we are interested. Whereas you, as a tourist – '

When they got back to the Green, Dunderdale made it plain that he was going not back to his home, but to church.

'Holy Communion?' he invited. 'It would give you an excuse for being out and about at this time of the morning.'

'You're an opportunist, Vicar.'

The only other communicant was the fat woman who had pounced on him in the Hall yesterday. After breakfast, the rain not having actually started again, he set out along the track behind the church; murky pools that had to be negotiated by way of sodden verges: the bole of a twisted old tree that drew its life-blood from a fissure between outcrops; more outcrops, until the landscape was nothing but outcrop, and he was walking tortuously between mossy limestone walls, as in a roofless cave.

He stood still for a moment and studied his surroundings. Here a shadower could easily make himself at home. There were huge trees, behind which a man could lurk at will, an expanse of wild raspberry canes, rambling over the dips of dead ground. Kenworthy listened: a drip of water into the carpet of dead leaves. And somewhere in the quarry ahead of him, he heard a living presence.

A large bird perhaps, foraging amongst the undergrowth? Or was it? This was something bigger, a reckless disturbance in the vegetation, and then a whimpering, hopeful at first, but rising to a desperate whine.

Kenworthy did not start to run. He walked on slowly, stopping every few yards: only a dripping here and there, as if the ghost of the departed rain were going to haunt the place for ever; a pause in the whining; and then a renewal of it, an orgiastic crescendo.

He came into the quarry. It was a small clearing, obviously not worked for many years. No commercial undertaking, this: only enough for a farmer to burn lime for his own fields and mend broken walls. The footpath entered the place through a narrow gully across which was stretched the disinterred root of a mountain ash. Enough to trip up a careless stranger, but nothing sinister about it. The root had not been freshly dug out: it had lain like that for a long time.

Kenworthy could place the animal now; a dog, higher up, well within the hollow of the quarry, making a vigorous exhibition of himself now he sensed a human presence: one of those animals that looked on all men as friends. Kenworthy skirted the inside face of the quarry, clambered over wet rocks, and came down to the wretched creature from above.

He was a mixture of breeds, fox-terrier an identifiable train, mostly white, with one black ear. He had been caught in a snare, a running-noose of nylon which had somehow drawn tight round a hock. The cord was anchored in three places, diabolically reinforcing each other; it could have held an Alsatian.

Kenworthy stooped to the knot, the animal lying confidently still. He was wet, shivering, had been out all night; but he was a resilient creature, and the moment he was released he started prancing enthusiastically. Kenworthy now started looking for another trap, the one that had been laid for the Colonel. It lay in the direct line that an impetuous rescuer would have taken up from the footpath. It was easy to find, crudely simple, an uneven weave of dead stalks and sere vegetation across a rock-strewn hollow some four feet deep.

Kenworthy plotted himself a wary course back through the quarry, stepped over the rowan root and began his return along the ravine, the dog at his heels. He drew in sight of the church and came back into the heart of the village. Across the Green he could see a knot of youngsters, girls and boys, congregated round a huddle of bicycles. There was no sign of their bus. Suddenly the dog left him, sprinted across to the group in frantic delight. He ran up to a slim girl: developing limbs under threadbare jeans. Davina: it was the first time he had seen her dressed in the contemporary idiom.

'Where've you been? Out all night! That's the first time you've ever done that to me!'

Then she saw Kenworthy.

'Oh, hullo. I've just heard you're going to be Wilbur. Isn't it marvellous?'

'Marvellous? I'm not so sure. In some frames of mind – '

'But you were so *sweet* on stage last night.'

'It's hardly the adjective I would have chosen.'

'Wasn't he?' she asked, and there was concerted agreement.

'Not at school?' he asked them generally.

'Half-term holiday. Just started.'

'And that's fine,' Davina added. 'You and I can get together for some private rehearsal.'

'I dare say I'll be glad of that,' he said, and there was a deep-throated, dirty laugh from some younger girl in the gang. Davina ignored it with the coolness of a party hostess.

'Actually, I was intending to come and see you this morning.'

'Well, do. My wife's probably out, but I know how to make coffee.'

'I think I'd better take this creature home first and give him something to eat. Where did you find him?'

'I was walking behind the church and he attached himself to me. Pretty fickle, though. He abandoned me as soon as he saw you.'

She bent down and mimicked anger with the dog.

'You'd better tell your mother you're going calling.'

'She won't mind. She'll be glad to have me out of the

house. I doubt whether she's up yet, anyway.'

Kenworthy went back to the cottage, and there was a
note from Elspeth saying that she'd gone to Derby with
two friends to help them buy stage cosmetics. There was
also a small rectangular package, *The Second Book of Hob*,
with Dunderdale's compliments. It aped the Gabbitas
original, except that the paper was glossier and the
letterpress less bold. The drawings might have come
from the same pen: little bearded, squinting men with
vulpine chins, going about their business as quarrymen,
cobblers and cowherds. The first story was about a *Hob*
innkeeper who diluted his beer.

Then he heard sounds of someone trying to enter the
cottage, apparently with violence, by the back door. He
went to unlock it before the ward could be broken from
the jamb, and found himself face to face with Mrs
Scadbolt, whose daily help he had firmly rejected.

'Ah, you had it locked, sir. I generally arrange with
people that they leave it undone, and then when they
want to go out for the day, and I'm on the late side, I can
still get in.'

'Yes, Mrs Scadbolt, but the only arrangement we had,
if I remember correctly, was that we shall regretfully not
be needing your services.'

Mrs Scadbolt's head bobbed; high scarlet cheek-
bones and a complex and unaesthetic superstructure of
black hair.

'Ah, yes, sir, but I did chance to meet Mrs Kenworthy
and she did happen to mention that she was getting so
tied up with things that she'd be glad of two hours three
times a week. Fifteen shillings an hour, sir, and she said
that you'd let me have it before I went.'

'I see. Well, in that case you'd better come in.'

Irony, since she was already in; but unappreciated.
She placed a basket in the middle of the table alongside
his book, which he scooped into his pocket.

'Brasso, sir, Windolene, new scrubbing brush, two dishcloths, twelve shillings altogether, sir. And may I have the Green Shield stamps, for going? Would you like to pay for the bits and pieces now, sir, then that's out of the way?'

She examined the cooker and made throaty noises about the boiling over of a pan of milk. Kenworthy retired to the sofa with the script.

'They tell me you made quite a hit in the Hall, last night, sir. Not that I agree with theatricals myself. I mean, don't you think it's bad for people, present company excepted, of course, sir, and it's different for you because I expect you're play-acting all day in your job. But take that girl, sir.'

She paused, possibly for breath.

'Now there's one I wouldn't care to leave *my* husband alone in a room with. And there's one or two homes I could mention where there's things would be flying about if half the truth were known. And that's saying nothing about what goes on with the Beaker Folk. That Mr Horrocks! Well, I've got a daughter in his class, and do you think it's right, sir, that children should be taught by a man who wears the sort of things he does? And the encouragement he gives that girl. It makes you think, doesn't it, sir?'

'I spend a lot of my time thinking about this, that and the other.'

'As for that Davina – '

She pronounced the name as if its very outlandishness was a moral outrage.

'I suppose we ought to feel sorry for her, and after all, I suppose it's in the blood. I said to my Mavis, look, you're both in the same class, so you've got to be sociable. But don't you go having more to do with her than you can help. And don't go getting asked round to her house. Not that anyone ever is. Ah, well, I suppose we ought to feel sorry for her.'

She had now finished with the cooker and was squeezing black exudations from a rag into the sink.

'How long have they lived here, the Stotts?' Kenworthy asked.

'Four years; no, five. I know because my Mavis – '

'They aren't village stock, then?'

'Oh, goodness, no. They're all Allsops or Brightmores in this village. Except for odd Scadbolts and Malkins who married one side or the other because they didn't know better.'

'I see. So who are their friends?'

'Ah, well, sir. There you've put your finger on it. I wouldn't say that Mrs Stott had any friends.'

'She doesn't mix with people?'

'You can hardly blame people for that.'

'I'm not blaming anybody, Mrs Scadbolt. I'm merely remarking that Mrs Stott does not appear to contribute to village life.'

'We ought to be grateful for small mercies. She doesn't *belong*, Mr Kenworthy, what with that *coat* and her *hair*, and she and that daughter of hers must live out of *tins*.'

It was the most commonplace words that carried her most melodramatic suggestions.

'And that Kevin O'Shea. Believe me, Mr Kenworthy, there are a lot of people in Spentlow, decent folk, who've slept sounder in their beds since you came here to keep an eye on things.' And in the same breath, 'There are others, I shouldn't wonder, who haven't slept a wink since you arrived.'

She paused for him to relish his unexpected effect on people's sleeping habits. He had just put his head back and closed his eyes when a tap on the door announced Davina. She had clearly used the dog's breakfast as a cover story for getting rid of the jeans image. These had now been exchanged for a canary yellow skirt and a green pullover over an orange blouse. She had combed out her hair so that one of her eyes was partially hidden.

She was wearing stiletto heels and false breasts. Seen at a distance, say on a street corner, a man might have been excused for mistaking her age and intention.

Kenworthy asked her in, and Mrs Scadbolt – who had amazingly now ceased to talk – did not turn round to look from whatever she was doing at the draining-board. Kenworthy offered the girl a seat. Mrs Scadbolt sniffed in such a way that one could not be certain whether she had sniffed or not.

'Actually,' Kenworthy said, 'I'm sure I shall appreciate the odd hour of extra practice. I shall need it. But I don't think there's much point in starting until I've got hold of more of the words.'

'I can help you to learn them.'

'There are certainly one or two stage directions I'd like you to put me right about.'

'I wouldn't pay too much attention to those. They're only what Mr Dunderdale wrote. John has changed things all over the place. Isn't your script absolutely covered with alterations?'

'No. Mine's a virgin copy.'

'Well, I've brought mine, so we can run over that.'

Mrs Scadbolt's back, now as expressive as her everyday vocabulary, looked as if she were prepared to spend the rest of the morning at the sink.

'I'll make coffee,' Kenworthy said.

That meant drawing water, for which he had to dislodge her.

'Mrs Scadbolt, I wonder if you'd mind leaving this room for the time being and just doing a general tidy-up upstairs?'

She walked away from him, her face expressively expressionless. Davina laughed, perhaps a trifle too noisily.

'Now, Davina – you told me you wanted to see me – '

She came and sat beside him on the sofa, her thigh warm and firm close to his. And yet her assumption of the position seemed so natural that there was even a suggestion of innocence about it. She was wearing a juvenile overdose of perfume. Kenworthy stood up.

'I'm frightened, Mr Kenworthy.'

There might have been footlights in front of them, for the infantile pathos she was registering.

'You mean frightened that someone does not want Gabbitas Week to go on?'

'Oh, that? Yes: someone is certainly trying to needle the vicar.'

'Needle the vicar? Someone has more than needled the Colonel.'

'Yes, it's terrible about Colonel Noakes,' she said, without feeling; the right thing to say, but she said it as if there were something radically missing from her powers of sympathy. Perhaps it was only due to her age. 'But it never occurred to me that it was anything but an accident.'

'There have been other accidents or near accidents.'

'But there's been nothing serious, has there? Mr Kenworthy, that isn't what I wanted to see you about.'

'No?'

'What's worrying me matters much more than Gabbitas Week.'

'Oh?'

'To me it does, anyway.'

Just the right touch of B-Film huskiness.

'It's my father,' she said, and looked at him for long enough for an audience to stop fiddling with their toffee-papers.

'Your father?'

Mrs Scadbolt had left the door open at the bottom of the stairs. Kenworthy crossed the room and shut it.

'Your father? Where is your father?'

'God knows.'

Tears not far away. Brave restraint.

'You'll have to begin at the beginning, Davina. I

haven't a clue about your family circumstances.'

He said this briskly and she looked at him with a pro-
gramme of facial expressions culminating in belated
understanding.

'Of course: how can you know? I am making the same
mistake that the rest of the village is. I suppose we rather
expect a man from the Yard to know everything. May I
ask you a question that I don't think you'll want to
answer?'

'Ask me anything you like.'

'Your visit to Spentlow – has it anything to do with the
Beaker Folk?'

'Would it worry you if it had?'

'Not at all. It's just that I made friends with a man
who wasn't very nice, that's all. But he's gone away now.
He didn't mean me any harm and he didn't do me any
harm. So please may I come back to the subject of my
father?'

'By all means.'

'I don't know where he is, Mr Kenworthy. The money
still comes through but – '

Mrs Scadbolt on the stairs; she held open the door
with her shoulder as she manoeuvred herself round it
carrying a bucket and broom. Davina showed herself
smart in conversational deception.

'Will you be word perfect in any scene by this evening,
Mr Kenworthy?'

'I doubt it. We'll have to run through it a lot before
I'm fluent.'

'That's what I find. I like to go for long walks running
over it in my head. I talk to myself along country lanes.'

'Good idea. I'm sure that hammers it home.'

'Perhaps we might go walking together.'

Mrs Scadbolt went and came through the back door.

'I'm not sure that would help much, Davina. I have
far more dialogue with the vicar than I have with you.'

'I've sat through so many rehearsals that I think I

know the vicar's part as well as I do my own. So shall we, Mr Kenworthy?'

'I think it might be a good idea. If the weather improves.'

'This afternoon?'

Mrs Scadbolt went back upstairs, this time leaving the door wider open than before. Kenworthy left it swinging.

'Not this afternoon, Davina.'

She looked at him with childlike disappointment.

'I need several hours alone with the script. You are forgetting what a raw beginner I am.'

'Tomorrow, then?'

Mrs Scadbolt called down the stairs.

'Would you like me to get fresh lining paper for these drawers, Mr Kenworthy?'

'Not today, Mrs Scadbolt,' and, 'Tomorrow's a possibility,' he said to Davina.

'I feel so frustrated, Mr Kenworthy.'

'We'll be meeting again at rehearsal this evening. We'll fix something then.'

Then wheels in the road outside: Elspeth arriving with her busy friends; an effusion of fixing to meet again this afternoon; a slamming of car doors, and Elspeth came in carrying a plastic bag full of super-marketing.

'Oh, hullo, Davina.'

Not frigid; not even positively cool, but short of welcoming.

'I've been discussing the play with your husband, Mrs Kenworthy.'

Spoken as if the child thought that Elspeth might mind.

Before lunch, he read another of the *Hob* stories: more spice for Spentlow readers. A Sopall had a field which he did not use. The down from its thistles blew gaily into the furrows of his neighbours. But when Hob's people wanted to buy it to make a playground for their children, the Sopall refused. Yet six weeks later he sold it, at three times the offered price, to a guild that wanted to build a rest home for retired locksmiths. This project had never materialized. In ten years the land had been put to no purpose and the thistles had multiplied an hundredfold. The tale was inconclusive.

CHAPTER VI

He spent the afternoon with the typescript.

My dear Vicar, she is not the slubberdegullion you take her for –

For the tenth time he had to turn to the script for the next line. He made himself a pot of tea. There was a walk that he wanted to make before first dark. Eventually he judged twilight far enough advanced, but not too far gone. He retrod the route that he had taken with Dunderdale this morning, passing the Stotts' bungalow, its curtains now open, but an uninhabited look about the house. In one window stood the triptych of a dressing-table mirror, its tea-chest plywood backing matt-painted and unvarnished. The strip of lawn was like a remnant of field: tall, seeded grasses, plantains, and irregular discoloured patches.

Sidi Barrani, on the other hand, suggested a frustrated gardener: pathetic care for a patch that was barely worth it: the autumn outgrowing of regimentally trimmed edges, the flowerless shrubs, punitively tonsured, in border soil almost too poor to sustain them. The news had come through that the Colonel had multiple fractures of femur and pelvis and had chipped three vertebrae. His condition was described as 'rather poorly'.

Kenworthy pressed on past Colonel Noakes's cottage. The lower end of the lane, where it tapered down to the so-called 'Roman' paving, was derelict and unobserved.

The lane was an access used by the farmer not more than two or three times a year. Kenworthy stooped and found that the base of the see-saw stone had been filled in again. Stones and loose clay had been packed back into place.

He turned to walk back to the village, past Sidi Barrani. And just as he was a few yards beyond the gate of the cottage he heard someone come out of its door. A bicycle passed him going up the lane, steering a weary course up the rough gradient, pedalled by a tall, thin woman in a drab brown coat.

Past the coarse fields, past the unconsoled-looking store cattle, past the Stotts' bungalow – or nearly past it. A pane in one of the front windows was lifted and Davina looked out.

'Mr Kenworthy – won't you come in and meet Mummy?'

She was still in the yellow, orange and green of this morning, or perhaps she had rushed back into it, having seen him go down the lane. She still had the hank of hair looped over one eye. He needed no second bidding.

He heard bolts being drawn, not easily: it was probably rare for the front door to be used. He stepped into a narrow and gloomy hall, heavy with stale furniture polish. There was dust on the telephone table, a strand of cobweb clinging to the flex that supported the Pre-Raphaelite hall-lantern.

'Mummy won't be a minute.'

Davina disappeared, having shown him into a diminutive sitting-room; hair cord carpeting, a shelf of book club editions that stopped short in the 1960s; a few pictures – surrealist horses and indigo elephants; a hockey stick in a corner, a guitar with two broken strings, a studio photograph of Davina at an earlier age, in pigtails, playing a recorder; but no sign or memento of any man; no radio or television; presumably the life of the bungalow was conducted over a kitchen table. There

were oddments of paper crumpled in the bare grate
behind a bar fire which had lost its plug: cannibalized, in
all likelihood, for some hair-drier or record-player.

There was a long delay before Diana Stott was ready
to appear. He heard her voice raised, wearily querulous,
but syllabically unintelligible; she hadn't taken kindly to
the *fait accompli* of a visitor. When at last she came into
the room, it was without a smile. She had blonde hair,
whose provenance was betrayed not only by the parting,
but by every furrow laid visible by hasty combing. She
was wearing a green woollen dress with a square of
cotton print knotted about her neck.

'Good afternoon, Mr Kenworthy. Please do make
yourself at home.'

She might have said something about being at sixes
and sevens, but less effectively tried to pretend that she
wasn't.

'May I make you a cup of tea? Or perhaps something
stronger?'

'It's early for anything stronger for me, Mrs Stott. A
cup of tea would be what they used to call grateful.'

Davina made no offer to go out and brew it; her
mother did not ask her to.

'I'll come and watch you make it,' Kenworthy said,
and lost no time in following her into the kitchen.

The room was cluttered. It was not poky as kitchens
go, but too small for two females to live in without strife.
There was a chair loaded with old periodicals. There
were a transistor radio and a rented television set. There
was a tradesman's calendar with milk deliveries
recorded in the margin. Beside the sink, among
unwashed crockery, a bowl contained the remnants of
breakfast cereal. A drawer was not closed properly, the
corner of a cleaning cloth sticking out of the top. An
electricity bill protruded from among old letters on top
of the ridge, in the red print that threatened power
cut-off.

'Davina tells me you're helping with the play, Mr Kenworthy.'

'In desperation they've asked me to try.'

She had nothing to say to this, gave the impression that she would rather not have been talking at all – better still that he had not been asked into the house. It had been mischief on Davina's part, inviting him; sheer mischief prompted by the desire for him to see what her mother was like.

'It will cause quite a stir in the village, the play,' he said.

'I dare say. Not much happens here.'

'So will the vicar's little book.'

She did not say anything to that. Her reaction would have been no different if she had never heard of *Hob* at all. She obviously knew next to nothing about the play. The biggest event in Davina's life, and they had not talked about it?

The kettle began its commotion and Mrs Stott flipped open the lid of a tea-caddy, closed her eyes, opened them, then closed them again in the direction of the ceiling.

'I'm sorry. We're out of tea-bags.'

'I told you last week,' Davina said.

'I'm sorry, Mr Kenworthy. Will instant coffee do? We don't drink much tea ourselves, and none of our friends do.'

'We have no friends,' Davina said, not quite inaudibly. A third mug had to be washed before there could be coffee.

There was no positive evidence that Diana Stott was an alcoholic. There were no bottles or used glasses about the room. But her eyes were certainly dull and baggy, and her hand had not seemed too firm while she was handling the kettle. She had spilled some water, but that was because the thing was too full, anyway.

Kenworthy took a bold line.

'I gather your husband's away, Mrs Stott.'

She raised clouded eyes and for the first time they held his.

'Do you blame him for that?'

A pause developed.

'I asked you a question, Mr Kenworthy. Do you blame a man for giving up?'

Unable to face her real enemies, whoever or whatever they were, she was ready to quarrel with the first comer. Even with Kenworthy. Davina turned her head away and let her lips spread in a supercilious smile.

'Oh, I don't know,' Kenworthy said. 'It looks a nice enough little place to me. Modern, convenient, labour-saving – '

'I wasn't talking about the house, Mr Kenworthy.'

'I can only talk about what I see with my own eyes, Mrs Stott.'

'Davina, go into your room for ten minutes. Go play a record or something.'

But the girl showed every sign of standing her ground. She was leaning against the sink with her coffee mug held at a casual angle. She looked into Kenworthy's face with amusement – satisfied amusement. On the point of provoking a stand-up row for his benefit? He signalled her out of the kitchen with a half-inch movement of his eyes. For a second or two it looked as if she was going to defy him. But then, meekly, shrugging her shoulders, perhaps out of nervousness rather than rudeness, she left them.

'Mr Kenworthy – may I ask whether you are here on duty?'

The mother spoke with more composure now, the first sign of relative independence he had seen in her.

'In Spentlow, do you mean, or in this house in particular?'

'Either or both. I think if you are, we have the right to know what you are about.'

'And what special reason do you have for thinking I might be on duty?'

'I suppose you're here to investigate these Beaker Folk.'

'Why should I be? Have you some complaint you'd like to lay against them?'

'No complaint that falls into the orbit of you people. Surely you know that that's half the trouble?'

'You're divorced, Mrs Stott?'

'He didn't want to know any more. He just couldn't take it. And I asked you just now: can you blame him?'

'I'm sorry. I wasn't clear what you meant.'

'She broke us up, and now she's breaking me down.'

'Then you just must not let her.'

'Her father has access, but he hasn't taken it up for a year or more. I don't blame him for that, either.'

'And it upsets her?'

She appeared not to hear that question.

'I had to take her to Child Guidance before she'd been at school very long. Before we came here. But it only made her worse. It was the last word in building up her importance. She was a perfect little angel in their office. All they did was give her a certificate to do as she pleased. And a note on the file – that they told her about – to say she's a near-genius. Licensed from then on to be an oddity.'

'Talented children are often difficult, Mrs Stott.'

'Difficult? Say impossible. Do you know that my husband and I didn't have an evening out together for four years because she played such hell with our baby-sitters? Do you know that she once unscrewed two stair-rods so that her father fell and broke his collar-bone?'

'But you still haven't told me why you think I should be professionally interested. Do you believe she has committed some crime? Or stands in moral danger?'

'I know next to nothing of what goes on in her life.'

'But you must suspect something, or you would not be talking like this.'

'I know she's fallen in with a bad lot. Or, rather, it's

them who have got into bad company. Hers.'

'So what is your worry, then?' he asked her. 'Drink? Drugs?'

'She doesn't like drink. She won't even touch a cigarette. Drugs – I have no fear of that. That's one of the strange things about her. In some things she seems to have all the sense in the world. But in other ways she never seems to learn. She gets mad notions into her head and goes through with them, irrespective of consequences.'

'For example, Mrs Stott?'

'For example, in the second school she went to she not only played truant. She even took a case full of clothes and changed into them in a public lavatory before she went off into town.'

'But that's a long time ago, Mrs Stott. Children grow out of that sort of naughtiness. If you could only tell me what you're afraid of today, this week, this minute – '

'I don't *know*, Mr Kenworthy.'

And then she was back again on the subject of the people at the Grange.

'These hippies, Mr Kenworthy. They are anarchists.'

'Ninety per cent of the riff-raff who call themselves that wouldn't have the guts to puff smoke at a gnat.'

'So, according to my ready-reckoner, there are ten per cent left. Davina's an anarchist too, so she tells me. An Ultimate Anarchist.'

'And what's that when it's at home?'

'Your guess is as good as mine. I can't tell you what it is that really frightens me. You must think I am out of my mind.'

'I don't think anything of the kind.'

The woman was weak, and from weakness had been buffeted into helplessness. There was no doubting the reality of her fear; no point in impugning her for not knowing what it was about. She made some effort to pull herself together.

'I'll tell you, Mr Kenworthy. You can think of me
what you like. Davina broke Donald and me apart. She
did it deliberately, schemingly, from the age of about
seven onwards. Looking back, I can think of dozens of
little things – devilishly clever things. We gave her everything she asked for, whether we could afford it or not. But
I know now that she had to destroy us. That's how her
mind works. When she sees something that makes
people happy, she has to destroy it. You'll think I'm
crazy, but I think she's set out to destroy these Ultimate
Anarchists too. Oh, I know they are dirty and feckless
and silly, full of their mad ideas. But they are trying to do
something, according to their own lights. That's why
she'll *have* to destroy them. I know her too well.'

It was real to her; and she was not strong enough to
handle it alone.

'Have you tried discussing it with anyone?' Kenworthy asked. 'The vicar, for example?'

'The vicar? If you ask me, he's an Ultimate Anarchist himself. He spends enough of his time up with that
crew.'

And that was more or less all there was to it. She was
no easier to convince than anyone else that he was only in
Derbyshire on holiday. He talked like a schoolmaster
and told her that if the crunch came and she happened
on something concrete she must go to the local police.
Then he let himself out of the back door, avoiding
another confrontation with Davina.

CHAPTER VII

When Davina Stott swept off her pixie cloak in the Hall
that night she was wearing her full costume and make-up
for the earlier phase of Gertrude Allsop. She had back-
combed her black hair and produced an elaborately

casual tangle that would go well with the muck-scattered farm-set. She had shadowed her eyes, brought up her lips into a frankly carnal invitation and was wearing torn rags with downward-pointing triangles that hung about her knees. She was bare-footed. There was no hint of immaturity or under-age pertness now. She was no longer the clever girl who was the only real actress in the village. She *was* Gertrude Allsop, and when she went for one of her contemporaries with a playful snarl and threatening claws, the illusion was gut-sinking. The only one who was displeased was John Horrocks, who showed purposeful irascibility.

'Davina, I told you we're not doing the farmyard scene again tonight. I want to introduce Mr Kenworthy to some of the other sequences.'

'I'm sorry. You know how it feels when you're looking the part.'

'That's not how Gertrude looked when she came back from her honeymoon. And that's what you're going to concentrate on tonight. Just imagine her turning up at a vicarage reception looking like that!'

'It might have been fun if she had.'

'Well, it isn't fun wasting our time. Go back-stage and get into something ordinary.'

'Where am I going to find something ordinary back-stage?'

'Go home and change, then. And please don't take all evening.'

For a moment she seemed to stand irresolute, on the brink of a prima donna fit. But then she thought better of it, came down the length of the auditorium blushing, unwilling to meet anyone's eye. It even looked as if she was going to cut Horrocks, but as she had almost passed him, she turned her head.

'Sorry, John.'

'All right, reverend gentlemen. Let's do your show-down again.'

So Kenworthy and Dunderdale went through the routine that they had done together last night, or, rather, they set out along the same lines. When Kenworthy found himself fluffing his words he started improvising along the broad scheme of the dialogue, and the vicar played up to him neatly, inventing on the spur of the moment lines that were a good deal better than some he had cooked up by the midnight oil. When it was over, John Horrocks was laughing. He looked as if he had been compensated for the passage with Davina.

'I can see that we're not going to have to spend much time rehearsing that one. But if that's the way you intend to play it, for goodness' sake remember that seven and a half minutes is the outside limit. Otherwise the interval tea's going to stew.'

And it was at this moment that a thousand-watt spotlight broke free from its clamp and came crashing down from the rafters. The bulb exploded like a cannon, the wrenched wiring flashed with blue and yellow lightning and blew a sub-circuit fuse that extinguished half the lights in the Hall. The lamp weighed thirty-five pounds, was too hot to touch, and took a chunk of flesh out of the shoulder of eight-year-old Susan Brightmore. If she had been standing six inches to her left, first-aid would have been superfluous.

As it was, the chaos was like a loose scrum. Too many people were trying to attend to the child; the haemorrhage was alarming. Too many people wanted to examine the fallen lamp. Children were crying; a teenage girl had fainted. Even the vicar's voice failed to rally the dissipated herd.

Then Horrocks called for his crowd scene, a popular event in the play. He got all his rhubarb-mongers on to the stage and thus off the floor. Elspeth and another woman were able to deal soberly with Susan Brightmore; and Kenworthy was looking over the electrician's shoulder at the spotlight.

'Someone ought to be shot in the county drama store, loaning stuff out in this condition. The bracket was practically shorn through.'

Kenworthy ran the tip of his finger over the torn metal. Then he slipped out and made the telephone call that one thing or another had caused him to put off.

When he returned, Davina was back in the Hall. She was wearing an austere two-piece costume in dove-grey and had put her hair up: a docile gesture, and an effect well suited to the scene they were going to play. She went and sat at the back of the room, swinging her legs from a perch on the Boys' Club vaulting-horse. Kenworthy lifted himself up beside her.

'What's an Ultimate Anarchist?' he asked.

She laughed with stage bitterness.

'It's obvious who you've been talking to.'

'Well, you set that up. What's an Ultimate Anarchist?'

She recited her answer like a well-drilled catechism.

'An Ultimate Anarchist believes that the height of moral perfection will be reached when life can be conducted without the need for external discipline of any kind, no rules, no exhortations even, no sanctions. The Ultimate Anarchist applies that principle to his own life, and strives by every non-violent means within his power to spread the pattern to the rest of society.'

'Bravo. And do you think that such idealism is worth pursuing, human nature being what it is?'

'I think that the earliest Christian churches came near to it. And the first settlers in Pennsylvania.'

'Inappropriate examples. In both cases they had rules and spiritual inspiration.'

'I said, came near to it.'

There was an impatient crack in her voice.

'Neither party succeeded in bequeathing either peace or saintliness to the next generation.'

'It takes time. Failure is no excuse for not trying again.'

'And that's what the Beaker Folk believe in? Indiscipline?'

'That's the wrong term for it.'

She was now angry with him.

'You say the same things that everyone else of your age-group does.'

'It seems to me too much like a damned good excuse for doing whatever you like,' he said.

'I don't think you've met any of the commune yet, have you? Except John?' She was still much put out, but then they were called on stage and played through their dialogue with reasonable efficiency. Kenworthy did not extemporize this time. He had made no pretence at learning anything from the later stages of the play, and kept his script in his hand. Davina was in crisp command of the character of the curate's young wife and gave him all the help he needed. But when Horrocks said, 'Cut, home and bed!' she walked away from Kenworthy as if their conversation on the vaulting-horse still rankled. Before he could isolate her in the still loosely-crowded room, the news was broken by someone who had just come in hot with it that Colonel Noakes had died in hospital earlier in the evening. Though not an old man, he had a constitution weakened by the deprivations of a prisoner-of-war camp and by a lifetime of lonely self-catering. He had been unable to stand up to pneumonia following secondary shock. Kenworthy began to pay very close attention indeed to Davina Stott.

She had got herself into a tight group of school-friends, with whom she had been laughing at nothing when the news was brought in. She heard it. They all heard it. And then, after a few subdued seconds, she was the one who started the conversation where it had left off. They were reminding each other of catch-phrases from a television situation comedy.

Colonel Noakes meant nothing to her at all; she did not pause to think of the passing of the man. Yet four nights ago she had been crouching under his knees, stroking his ribs under his pullover, not stopping to think what a sport he was to let himself in for it. Kenworthy came up behind her.

'I'll walk you home, Davina.'

For seconds it looked as though she was going to snub him.

'You and I have a conversation to finish. We were not making much progress, remember, under the eagle eye of Mrs Scadbolt.'

She turned to him then with her most angelic of smiles. It was similar to the way in which she had reacted to Horrocks's rebuke. It seemed that when she had been in the wrong she could snap out of her mood suddenly, behave as if it had never happened, could perhaps even convince herself that it hadn't. It was as if she had not even remembered.

'Good idea. If there's anyone else down our lane tonight, they'll be too wrapped up in their own affairs to be eavesdropping.'

She took his arm as they left the grounds of the Hall, leaned her head for a moment against his shoulder, as if they were Gertrude and Gabbitas, then straightened herself up, said, 'This won't do, will it?' and walked respectably enough at his side.

'*I don't like that hat-stand,*' she said. '*There was one in a furniture shop in Scarborough I fancied, but I did not see how we would ever get it home.*'

'*But we are living in the nineteenth century, dear girl. If you saw one in Outer Mongolia that appealed to you, I would have it brought to Spentlow.*'

Thus reciting, they pulled themselves away from the crowd. As they were approaching the narrow entrance to the lane, beyond the pool of light from the last of Spentlow's few lamps, she began to lean against him again. He put her gently away.

'We are not blind beggars, afraid that we might get lost. I'd better warn you that I am one of those people who have rather a horror of physical contact.'

'Like Lawrence of Arabia?'

'Let's say the comparison ends there.'

'You're not doing so badly in the play.'

'Let's forget the play for ten minutes. You were telling me this morning how worried you were.'

'Ah, yes.'

'Well, are you? Or aren't you?'

'Don't sound so severe, Mr Kenworthy. Of course I am worried. Daddy doesn't answer my letters. He has access once a month, but he no longer comes for me. He doesn't remember my birthday. I just can't make contact.'

'You haven't done anything to upset him?'

'She did cover a lot of ground with you this afternoon, didn't she?'

'I always listen to both sides. Now I'm listening to yours. And if I ask blunt questions, it's because I want unembroidered answers. That's my way, and if you don't like it, you'd better not come to me with your troubles.'

'Sorry, Mr Kenworthy.'

'Has he another lady-friend, perhaps? Is he thinking of marrying again? Maybe someone who wouldn't want to be strung up with his past?'

'Daddy won't marry again. The way Mummy saddled him with maintenance, he couldn't afford to keep two homes. I don't know how he manages the one and a half that he's stuck with at present. That's what it amounts to. He's in a bed-sitter. And I may say I'm costing him a pretty penny myself.'

'Are you proud of that?'

'Why do you say things in that tone of voice, Mr Kenworthy?'

He ignored the question.

'You said this morning that his money is still coming through?'

'It has to. It's paid through the court.'

'And why did they break up?'

'Marriage hopelessly on the rocks. Mummy drank. She's been dried out three times. Always at Daddy's expense. In clinics. Once even since they parted; she always goes back to it. She always will.'

They had drawn abreast of her bungalow now. No sign of the light or life. Kenworthy led her further down the lane, towards Sidi Barrani.

'She's an alcoholic – and yet she got custody of you?'

'Daddy's too much of a gentleman. He took the blame for their failure. Admitted mental cruelty. Sometimes I think he really believes it was his fault.'

'It takes two to make most situations. And you don't think that you yourself might have contributed to their troubles? You have to agree that it could be on the cards.'

'It *is* on the cards. It was true. I was a little bitch sometimes.'

An odd confession; sudden and factual, without tone of remorse. It might be because she knew how to win and hold attention.

'But I've learned better now.'

'Does your mother think so?'

'Oh, *her* – !'

'She *is* an interested party.'

They had now reached the Colonel's cottage, and Kenworthy still went on walking, down towards the 'Roman' paving. She seemed to show reluctance to come with him, but stayed at his elbow. When they reached the spot where the Colonel had fallen, he began shuffling his feet. He drew his torch suddenly out of his pocket and shone it on the ground. The beam spread over the stone in an elongated oval.

'I don't think you liked playing Gertrude to Colonel

Noakes's Gabbitas, did you?'

'Not half as much as I do with you, that's for certain. He should never have been asked to do the part. Oh, don't think I'm not sorry about what happened to him. But he was ruining the play.'

He showed her the place where the stone had been tampered with.

'Somebody did this with a trowel. Someone who lived near at hand, I think – near enough to slip back here and fill it in again. It was your dog that someone fixed into a snare. He didn't get into it himself. Someone tied a knot in two tufts of grass. Someone who likes taking country walks?'

'I don't know what you're getting at, Mr Kenworthy.'

'I'm suggesting that there are some people who would go to any lengths, even to get something trivial, if they wanted it badly enough.'

He stopped talking, and she was in no hurry to puncture the silence. For seconds they stood motionless, half turned to each other. Then she came smartly to life and turned away from him.

'Please let me go home. I'd hate to be someone you seriously suspected, Mr Kenworthy.'

'You're a strange girl, Davina.'

'And not a very happy one,' she said. 'I must go now.'

She began to walk up the lane. He walked a yard or two from her and they did not linger outside her gate.

Elspeth had already gone to bed when he got in. She was lying on her side with the sheets pulled up over her cheeks. He quietly emptied his pockets into the drawer of his bedside table. But she was not asleep. The onslaught started abruptly. She was primitively angry.

'Where have you been?'

'Exploring. Seeing a young lady home.'

'Are you out of your senses?'

'No – merely reeling a little.'

'You know that that girl has a crush on you?'

'Is that the opinion of the Amalgamated Ladies of Spentlow?'

'It's the opinion of my own eyes and ears. She's making a set at you, and a man of your age and experience ought to have seen it.'

'I doubt if any crush will have survived what I said to her just now.'

'You're falling into the very trap that catches the most reasonable of men. You let yourself feel flattered by her attentions. I suppose you're at what they call the dangerous age. And I'm sorry if I've not been feeling too – '

'If you had heard our line of talk – '

'The last I saw of you, you were crossing the Green like a couple from Hardy: "Yonder a maid and her wight – " '

'That was before I told her I can't stand physical contact.'

'So what have you been doing all this time?'

'Showing good reason why I might suspect her of murder.'

'What?'

'Just made her think. I don't think I did any harm. The local police will be here in the morning. I've telephoned them. I'll be glad to have it out of my hands.'

'You really think that that child – ? Well, of course, you can't call her a child – '

'She's a child, right enough, in a number of ways. A clever one. A consummate actress and an intuitive manipulator of people. She likes the limelight – she *must* have it. Must be different, must be distinguished. It doesn't always come off, so she's what's known as mixed up. Her mother had her at Child Guidance Clinics before they came here.'

'I didn't know that.'

He had taken off his shirt and vest and went out to

wash. When he came back, Elspeth was motionless again. But again she pulled the bed clothes away from her face.

'Go on.'

'She's mixed up, as most kids are at some time or other. But she doesn't sort herself out as most kids do, which is by practical compromise. She can't do that, because she's too positive. Getting yourself unmixed – we've all had to do it at some time or other – is the process of socialization, adapting to your environment. Davina can't adapt. Her ego won't let her. When her ego is threatened – I saw it happen just now, when John Horrocks ticked her off for exhibitionism – she sometimes retreats. But there are times when she can't. All this, by the way, is pure hypothesis. Let's call it Possibility One.'

'And Possibility Two?'

'That's she's a psychopath.'

'I'm never quite sure what that word means.'

'What Davina Stott is.'

'Try again.'

'Then let's say she's plain evil.'

'Emotive and unsatisfactory. Define your terms.'

'By evil I mean absence of good.'

'That's just begging the question.'

'Let's beg it, then. Daniel Dunderdale would be more categorical, but I'd rather steer clear of his specialized terms. Let's say Davina Stott is evil. She knows what good is, but she rejects it. A lot of people do; that's how I come to earn a pay-packet at the end of each month. But in the case of most people, being good is a pretty superficial business. It means keeping out of trouble; you adapt to society, but you keep an eye open for society's weaknesses. It goes deeper than that with Davina Stott, because she's positive about evil, too. It's not just that she doesn't choose to be good. She hates good. So whenever she sees it she sets out to destroy it.'

'That's making a devil of her.'

'Now we are back into Dunderdale's world. If you'd seen her callousness about the Colonel, you might have believed it. Her mother says she destroyed their marriage; and that woman has been destroyed by something. Why do you think she loves playing Gertrude Allsop? Correction, loves *being* Gertrude Allsop? Because Gertrude Allsop ultimately destroyed Wilbur Gabbitas; destroyed him because she had come to hate a goodness that she could not match. Is that such a long march to Davina destroying the play? Her mother believes she's going to destroy the Beaker Folk.'

'I hope you're wrong, Simon. She might try to destroy you, next. What's your state of aversion to physical contact?'

'Amenable.'

'Put your arm round me.'

Sleep came hard to him. At two o'clock he drew away from Elspeth. Without putting on the light he found his way across the room, took his dressing-gown from the bedroom door, and went down the stairs as silently as the abused treads would tolerate.

On top of the bookcase downstairs were Elspeth's notes on the life of a CID wife. He did not read them, but his eye could not help catching the top sheet. She had divided her talk into two parts: 'What he tells me?' and 'What I am left thinking'. He put the kettle on and settled down to make notes to pass on to his Derbyshire colleagues.

Half past four was upon him when he looked again at the clock. He did another stint at learning the script, and applied himself to the last scene. Gertrude had become more and more restless as she aped the superficialities of the curate's wife's world. There were times when even Gabbitas's love for her became exasperated, times when the couple quarrelled, when Gabbitas could not escape from his own orthodoxy. Suddenly, Gertrude had vanished from home, had hidden herself irretrievably back among her familiar hills. On one of the parlous smallholdings she had taken up with some cousin, also an Allsop, a quasi-savage recluse, a man of crude appetites as insatiable as her own.

Gabbitas had pined for her, had sought her in vain amongst the sterile crags and the valleys, frustrated and tricked at every turn by the freemasonry of the hill-folk. Never a strong man, his constitution sapped by the midnight oil and closed garrets of his youth, his will to resist infection dissolved. He succumbed to the consumption that set red spots burning high on his cheek-bones.

When she heard of his death, Gertrude saw all things clearly. She came back to Dogtooth to seek spiritual refuge with her father; but old Reuben would not let her in. The last tableau of the play saw her writhing hysterically on the stolen threshold of the farm – the Anathema Stone itself.

At a quarter to five Kenworthy drew back the living-room curtains. The world was invisible in black night. He opened the window a couple of inches, and a cold draught blew in. He went back to the sofa, exchanging the script for the new book of *Hob*: a naive and not very amusing yarn about an irresistible Sopall and an immovable Glitter-Better. A cosmic parallelogram of forces had sent them both off along a lethal diagonal.

Then footsteps ran the length of the village. He looked at the time: seventeen minutes past five. Someone was running inefficiently, hindering himself by attempting a speed that was beyond him. Kenworthy heard him stumble, thought he had fallen, but the footsteps picked up their rhythm again. He went to the window, but could see nothing: a close-blanketed night, as yet not a niggardly breakthrough of grey.

The runner came nearer. He was going to pass the house. But a second before he put his hand on the gate fastening, Kenworthy knew that this was where the man was coming. Kenworthy moved silently into the hallway, put up his hand to the latch and had the door open while the man was still in the act of knocking. It was the vicar, the vicar hatless, his cloak askew about his shoulders. And the vicar was in distress, the distress of a man who has been mobbed or ambushed, the breathlessness of a man carrying too much weight for sporadic athletics.

'Come inside. What on earth – Are you hurt?'

Dunderdale was in a filthy condition, daubed with mud and muck, his clothes soaked, as if he had struggled through a weed-choked autumn ditch. Already a light was on upstairs. Elspeth came down, hair dishevelled, in her pink dressing-gown.

'Why, Vicar – what on earth?'

'Come with me, Kenworthy.'

'Just put me in the picture.'

'I'll make a hot drink,' Elspeth said.

'There's not time.'

'Just get out of those things.'

'Later – Kenworthy, come with me.'

'I'll get dressed.'

Two and a quarter minutes, it took him, shoes patiently tied. Dunderdale was now sitting on one of the hall chairs, on to which Elspeth had coaxed him. He shot up again at the sound of Kenworthy's feet on the stairs.

The vicar wanted to run again, but Kenworthy held him to his own fast walk.

'Just give me the essentials.'

'You'll see for yourself, not two minutes from here.'

'This is no time for play-acting, Vicar.'

'We're not play-acting. By God, we're not.'

Down an entry between walls, boggy patches, ankle-deep; press on – through a gate held by a loop of leather, into a typical Spentlow yard, with its stinks, its filth, its creatures fractiously startled from sleep. Dogtooth: Jesse Allsop's.

'It was Allsop who came to fetch me,' Dunderdale said. 'Pity he didn't think of fetching you, too. He had to get up in the night. That's how he saw – '

There were lights on all over the farmhouse, the door widely ajar, the man who must be Jesse Allsop coming out to meet them. A Tilley lamp, hissing, unnaturally bright, had been placed out on the cobbles in the yard; not too close, as if with a suggestion of respect for what lay across the doorstep: the Anathema Stone. It wouldn't have been a man's first reaction that the form had ever sparkled with life. But Kenworthy recognized the costume of someone in whose company he had been acting a scene something like seven hours ago. The appalling corpse had been Davina Stott.

Part Two

CHAPTER VIII

Jesse Allsop was short, stocky, but lacking the physical strength that is kept in trim only by application. He had not done that kind of work for twenty years. Dark-eyed, dark-visaged, like his half-savage ancestor, he had little to say, not out of sullenness, but out of a lifetime of distrusting speech. Yet he had also an ingrained preference for the unobtrusively conventional. At some hour of the night he had changed into a sombre, anciently worn but evidently respected working suit, and his hair, lacking any hint of grey even at the temples, was sleeked down, suggesting a throw-back to the nineteen-thirties.

There was polish in the house, and no dust. At half past eight each morning, a woman came over from the village to do for him, by which time he had cooked, eaten and cleared his own breakfast. The room in which he received Dunderdale and Kenworthy was proud in the affluence of a departed era: heavy furniture, too much of it. On the wall was a large, late-century photograph of a not-very-intelligent matriarch, but one with a mind of her own, however limited; eyes not open to interpretation, but committed to their own memories; Reuben Allsop, relenting on his death-bed, had bequeathed to Gertrude his considerable capital gains, and she had come down to Dogtooth with the son she had had by her cousin.

Jesse Allsop had given up farming, except that he still lived in this house and probably could not tolerate living anywhere else. The work in the yard, which stopped strictly at his door, was done by a neighbouring relative, to whom the land was leased. The room, for all its period pieces, was dominated by a television set with a twenty-six-inch screen. A desk calculator was lying casually on a side table, and the telephone was a prestige model.

Jesse Allsop had seen, a crucial few years before most of the others, that the returns from hill-farming were not worth the grind. The slopes were too scraggy here for the profitable herds that were feeding the Stilton factory at the head of the dale. It was natural beauty that the discontented Midlanders and Northeners were prepared to pay money for, happy to find temporary footing on High Peak soil. Jesse Allsop owned eighty caravans on the edge of this and other villages dotted about the flanks of Dove and Manifold. He had thirty letting cottages, all nominally furnished. He smiled wryly when men told him that word of mouth was the best advertisement; he did not care what went from mouth to mouth. It did not matter to him if the same family never came twice to his roof-trees. There were tens of thousands more where the first few hundreds had come from.

'At what time did you call the police?'

And Allsop looked at Kenworthy as if he thought him demented.

'What do you mean? You *are* the police.'

Kenworthy reached for the telephone.

'My name is Kenworthy,' – no rank, no explanations – 'I am speaking from Dogtooth Farm, Spentlow, the residence of Mr Jesse Allsop. There has been a violent death on the premises. I shall remain here until someone arrives.'

In an armchair the vicar was leaning back inelegantly; filthy, dog-tired, tormented by revulsion now that the spring of instant activity was uncoiled. It was an act of moral cruelty not to let him go home, get stripped, bathed and to bed, but Kenworthy had put himself in charge.

'I have no standing at all in the activity that's going to buzz about here in an hour's time. It would be wrong of me to interfere, would confuse the issue. I shall merely assume the minimal functions of scene-of-crime officer until the real man arrives.'

They had come indoors and sat waiting, no one attempting to make conversation, least of all Jesse Allsop. At ten minutes to seven they heard someone handling the fastening of the yard gate. Kenworthy hurried out. A grey shadow of a man was letting himself in; the tenant farmer. There was an anticipatory stir in a cowshed, and an animal lowed.

'Don't come any further, please.'

'Who are you? And who do you think you are ordering about?'

'I am a police officer. There has been trouble. I'm allowing no one to enter until my colleagues arrive.'

'I've got to see to the cows.'

'Come back in an hour.'

Then the man caught sight of what was lying across the stone. He would be the first to set up rumours in Spentlow. It hardly mattered. There was little point in delaying them.

The grey day was lightening now. Dunderdale came out of the house.

'No point, you think, in getting down to work while the trail is still hot?'

'I don't know whether it's hot, or was ever hot, or cold, or will ever be anything but cold. It's important for me to do nothing.'

'In that case, please let me go home. When they want me, I'll not be five minutes' walk away.'

'I need you here. You're a man of standing. I shall need you to swear to my actions – or, rather, inertia – since I arrived on the scene.'

'Why should that be necessary?'

'Because it complicates a case when a man like me is a primary suspect.'

'You, a suspect?'

'I must be. Statistics show, our procedures acknowledge, that in the majority of cases a murderer turns out to be one of two people: the one who found the victim dead, or the last one to see him alive.'

'Statistics – '

'I am determined to stick to the manual.'

They were joined now by Allsop, who came gloomily out of his door, his arms swinging loosely in front of him. The Tilley lamp was still hissing, its light now superfluous. Allsop took a step towards it.

'Leave it. Let it burn itself out.'

'Oil costs money.'

'Weigh that against how many years that girl might have had in front of her.'

'I put it there. I've trodden the ground already.'

'And the man with his head full of footprints is going to say you were one too many.'

Now Allsop did begin to sulk. And beyond the lamp the dove-grey costume looked pathetically cheap.

Davina Stott was lying full length, her limbs at inhuman angles. The side of her face was against the barrow stone and a tress of her hair was still stirring silkily. Her right arm was doubled unnaturally beneath her.

'Did you touch her?' he asked Dunderdale.

'I tried to turn her over as well as I could with my torch battery running out. How was I to know that she was beyond help?'

'Of course you didn't.'

Kenworthy suddenly became gentle, consoling. He looked round the yard, the first time he had taken it all in by daylight: the paraphernalia of subsistence farming, a broken root-cutter, the windlass of an abandoned well, a pump in a corner – the one they had been at such pains to represent in their stage set. When it came to scenes of crime, the manual teetered on the brink of self-conscious poetry. The scene of a crime was a place that had been visited, however fleetingly, by the man who had committed that crime. And wherever a man goes he leaves some trace of his passage, however slight, however invisible to the untrained eye.

'Ought we not go and tell Mrs Stott?'

'Do you think she's awake yet? Do you think she's still waiting up for the girl? Do you think it's the first time she's been out all night?'

And Kenworthy turned to Allsop.

'I'd like you to run your eyes over the yard – no, from where you're standing. Tell me if anything's been moved since yesterday.'

Allsop did as he was asked, perfunctorily.

'Do you think I know all that's in the bloody yard? Every time I cross it, I try not to look at it.'

'Did you know this girl, Mr Allsop?'

'Vaguely.'

'How vaguely?'

'She did some work for me the summer before this. Holiday work – several of the kids do: cleaning up the vans on a Saturday, when the new trippers arrive. She came up here.'

'What for?'

He did not look the sort of employer who kept open house to his work-force. 'She said she'd been paid two pounds short over the season. I didn't argue.'

'Just peeled them out of your wallet?'

'No: told her to bobby off. That's what I call not arguing.'

'That's not the whole truth, Jesse.' Dunderdale had come to life, but not with much energy. It was a mechanical rebuke, like a mother correcting the narrative of a child.

'You know very well she was up here two or three times a week at that time.'

'Trying it on. She got no two quid out of me.'

'Mr Kenworthy – Jesse is by no means the curmudgeon he would have you believe. He has himself to thank for his public image.'

'A man could make his own image, if some people would let history die.'

'History can never die, Jesse – "unto the third and fourth generation". '

'That is the old law, Vicar. Don't you preach that it has been fulfilled?'

'That depends on which law men choose to live by.'

'If you hadn't chosen to put on your damned Gabbitas Week, a lot of things were on their way to being forgotten.'

'And only injustices remembered? Gabbitas Week will wipe out a tangle of misunderstandings.'

'And I say you're wrong, Vicar. You're doing the village a disservice. Spentlow's becoming a new place. Let the process work itself out.'

'Will Spentlow ever change while it's full of Allsops and Brightmores? Did you know that Barton Brightmore has helped himself to your cloak-tree?'

'You think I care? You think it matters to me who has it?'

'It matters to Barton Brightmore and his following. But I've everything lined up for him. He'll get the shock of his life, come Gabbitas Week.'

'Gabbitas Week? You're still thinking of having a Gabbitas Week – after this?'

Then they heard a car engine coming up the Spentlow street; the change into low gear as it scouted past farm entries; the reverse turn; the jolting along ruts. The scene-of-crime car arrived first, a beefy and beery young inspector with one detective-constable, both of whom clearly knew what they were about. A brief look at the corpse – the inspector might have been a batsman at the wicket, surveying the field as of habit. Then the marker tape was being laid out, laying down the no-go area. Within minutes a bigger car was parking behind the first, three men this time, their obvious master a man in his early forties, with clipped fair hair that still had enough spirit of independence to react in the slight breeze. It gave him a misleadingly boyish look. Chief Inspector Michael Gleed; Kenworthy neither knew him nor of him. At least he made some kind of noise in his throat, as he viewed the body. Then he listened to Kenworthy as an overworked doctor might hear the first recital of symptoms from a new patient.

Then factual statements: Allsop's first, because he had been the first to see the body. He had got up to urinate, had seen what he had seen, had gone close enough to the corpse to know that it was a corpse, had not touched it. He had gone in and dressed, then went for the vicar, lighting the Tilley lamp when he came back. Why the vicar? Because the vicar knew the girl. Because the vicar was the natural intermediary with the Scotland Yard man who was staying in the village.

Why had he not rung direct to the police? Well, they'd got the police here, hadn't they? He did not add that the indirect approach helped to soften reality. Calling in Kenworthy had about it a touch of keeping things in the family.

Next, Dunderdale: he had been in bed when Allsop came to his door. It was about half past four, but he was still reading. The evening's rehearsal had left him excited and tense; he was often awake half the night. He had hurried with Allsop to Dogtooth. He had to admit that he had disturbed the body; it was a reasonable thing to do, wasn't it, to see if there was anything left to resuscitate? Then he had gone for Kenworthy – obviously, with such eminence on tap. He knew that Kenworthy had no status in the area, but Kenworthy would know what to do, wouldn't he? Besides –

Gleed was not the man to miss an inflection, particularly the hint that here was a line that a man was already wishing he had not broached.

'Mr Kenworthy already knew something of the girl's background.'

Kenworthy did not intervene. His turn came. He was Detective-Superintendent Simon Kenworthy. He was holidaying in Spentlow: well, trying to. He'd agreed to help out with amateur dramatics, and in that sphere he had on two or three occasions met the girl whose body lay out there. He had, in fact, walked her home after rehearsal. He had seen her as far as her gate, had watched her go through it, had heard her footsteps go up to her front door as he himself was returning up the lane. Time? It was twenty past eleven when he arrived back at his cottage. It had been a long rehearsal, had it? Well, it had gone on until half past ten. They must have found plenty to talk about afterwards, Gleed said, suppressing innuendo. Well, the girl was mixed up; there'd be more to say about that later. It was undoubtedly better not to clutter up an initial statement with secondary stuff. Kenworthy was at Gleed's absolute disposal, wasn't going anywhere, wasn't doing anything – except, as an immediate priority, sleeping.

Gleed clicked the retractable tip of his ballpoint – a silver Parker – slipped it back into his pocket, looked down for a fraction of a second to see that the clip had gone home: a man methodical in detail.

'One more question at this stage.' Gleed was a quiet man, no drama, cold emphasis in his clarity.

'You haven't mentioned notifying the girl's parents.'

'Professionally indefensible. I'd have had the lights out of a subordinate who had tripped up on that one. But there's only the mother, she's divorced. There'd have been no point at all. Wakes about ten, I imagine – and can't do much with her hands till she's had her first noggin.'

Gleed said nothing.

'I restricted myself to keeping Dunderdale and Allsop where I could see them, and ensuring that nothing was touched in the yard.'

Gleed did not react at all. The inspector outside was already labelling finds in little plastic bags. Gleed was paying as much attention to him at a distance as he was to Kenworthy close at hand.

Fatigue was invading Kenworthy in a wave that began with a prickling somewhere in the lumbar region, and that crept up his spine until he had to halt in his steps and take in deep breaths of the sharp air. It was still early morning. Spentlow was still coming out of its night. Bedroom curtains were being snatched open: they didn't know yet. They couldn't. Or had Spentlow its own herd perception, that would not need telling?

Elspeth saw the fatigue in his face and refrained from asking questions. She cooked him the sort of breakfast he had written home about from country pubs in his journeyman days. Fatigue left it half-finished. Elspeth put him to bed; and then the tensions of fatigue drove sleep away, so that he got up again and came down for a notebook, determined not to be found unready when the time came.

CHAPTER IX

Kenworthy slept, an unfightable sleep that mastered him while he was still labouring over his notes; then he woke and scribbled a word or two more; and finally a deeper sleep won, and he dropped his notebook, and his pen rolled away amongst the cloughs and dales of the eiderdown. It was a quarter to midday when Elspeth woke him, with a steaming black coffee on a tray.

'They're here, Simon. Your Derbyshire colleagues. Or at least, one of them is.'

He heard her talking after she had gone downstairs again.

'He's surfaced. Give him five minutes. He was up all night.'

Kenworthy took one sip of his coffee, then went downstairs in his dressing-gown. The man who was waiting for him was young and trendy: shirt with wide stripes and a large unshapely collar, hair in an outgrown Beatle cut.

'Sergeant Cottier.'

'Kenworthy.'

'I'm here about your complaint.'

Complaint: his suspicions about Noakes's death ranked officially as a crime complaint. There was some humming and ha-ing, the sergeant coming in with cross-questions because Kenworthy was going too fast. As can happen in the most efficient of forces, especially a big one, there had been a near snarl-up. This man had left his HQ this morning with the Kenworthy assignment on his clip, two other jobs to do first, and no knowledge of the other report that had come in from Spentlow.

'Sorry, Sergeant. I'm usually able to make myself clearer than this, I hope. I think you'd better slip down the road and see your Chief Inspector Gleed, before we get any lines crossed.'

'Gleed? What's Gleed doing here?'

Kenworthy told him. The sergeant shut his book.

'Where am I likely to find him?'

In the early afternoon Kenworthy, shaved and dressed, tried to settle on the sofa with the third of his novels: a paperback that had been runner-up for a national award. After the first three pages he threw it across the room. Elspeth suggested that a walk would do him good, but he said that he could not leave the house with Gleed likely to arrive at any moment. Supper was already on the table when the Chief Inspector came.

He still looked younger than his years, which made his real years look light for the rank that he carried. He apologized for coming at a meal-time.

'There are one or two points.'

'Fire away.'

'According to your statement, you were talking to Davina Stott for close on an hour after rehearsal.'

'That would be about right.'

'And earlier in the evening you had put in a crime complaint.'

'In the public interest.'

'Suggesting that the death of Colonel Noakes was not accidental.'

'I am sure it was not. I have prepared a statement of my full reasons for thinking so.'

'Presently. You did not make your phone call until after the Colonel had actually died.'

'When I rang I did not know he was dead.'

'Previously, you had rung a colleague at Scotland Yard with information about a character called Kevin O'Shea. I may say that, as is only right and proper, the Met. passed your item on to us for comment. What I am trying to say is this: if you've been privateering on our pitch, that's a matter between your bosses and mine. But it's got to be cleared up before I can go any further.'

'I am not and have not been privateering. I have no commitments here. I am here for relative solitude and rest.'

'So where does O'Shea come into it?'

'I heard him mentioned as prominent in a commune that has been squatting here in Spentlow Grange since the spring. I happened to have heard his name and description at the Yard – canteen talk. I can't even remember the context, but I know that my friend Detective Inspector Clingo badly wanted to question O'Shea.

The description fitted. So I passed on what I'd heard.'

'And the Stott girl was involved with O'Shea?'

'I don't know. I know she had got in with the crowd at the Grange. How deeply, and with which individuals, I can't say. I saw enough of her to know that if there was a spurious minority setting up shop on her doorstep, she'd at least take a look.'

'Is that what you were talking to her about late last night?'

'No. I was bullying her. There had been so many incidents connected with the vicar's play that I thought there was a *prima facie* case for suspecting sabotage. I believe that Colonel Noakes died as a result of one of those incidents.'

'You'd better give me the details.'

Kenworthy did. And Gleed listened without expressing an opinion.

'And you believed that the girl was involved?'

'I thought it was worth a probe. She was unmoved by the Colonel's death.'

'You accused her – by implication, at least?'

'She saw which way my mind was working.'

'Pushing it a bit, weren't you?'

'If I'd been on duty, I fancy I'd have played it about the same.'

'If you'd been on duty, you'd have lost no time in informing her mother of her death.'

'On the contrary, I'd have done just what I did: put the security of scene of crime first.'

Gleed was not being hostile. But his questions were incisive.

'You questioned Mrs Stott yesterday afternoon, I believe.'

' "Questioned" is pulling the angle a bit. The girl had asked me in to meet her.'

'Why should she do that?'

'Part of her habit of dramatizing everything. Chief

Inspector, I have been helping out with a part in a play – in an emergency created by the Colonel's accident. The girl and I played a number of major scenes together. She was an intelligent child with something of a flair for the stage. She was able to give me a good deal of help, things I'd missed from previous rehearsals. She'd also talked to me about some of her personal worries; particularly a cooling-off of her father's attitude to her.'

Kenworthy summarized everything that had passed between him and Davina. Gleed had to keep slowing him down so that it could all go into his notes.

'Tell me again the circumstances in which you actually said goodnight to her.'

'I think she was more angry than shaken at what I'd actually said to her. She said she wanted to go in. I walked her up to her gate and left her there. I heard her go up the path to the house, but by the time she had reached it I was well up the lane.'

'You did not hear any banging, as if she'd been locked out?'

'There was none. I can be sure of that.'

'No scene outside her mother's bedroom window?'

'No such thing. I could not have missed it.'

'Your impression is, then, that she went into the house?'

'I had no reason to think otherwise. I did not give it any thought. Certainly it did not occur to me that she might have been locked out. If you'd asked me, I'd have said she had her own latch-key.'

'She did not call up the lane after you?'

'I'd be bound to have heard her.'

Gleed went on in a matter-of-fact tone: one professional sharing material fact with another.

'She *was* locked out. Her mother had bolted and chained the door, and, as far as we can tell, had gone to bed in a virtual coma.'

'I can believe that. But I have no idea how the girl

reacted. I doubt whether it was the first time it had happened to her. I don't know what sheds they have – '

'None.'

'Then she must have remained quietly under the eaves of the bungalow, waiting for me to be out of earshot.'

Gleed looked at him sharply.

'Why should she do that?'

'Partly so as not to prolong conversation on an awkward topic. Also perhaps so that I would not know what was to be her next port of call.'

'Do you think that bothered her?'

'I think she was a girl with all sorts of guilt mix-ups.'

'You wouldn't have expected her to call on your help?'

'Well, anyway, she didn't.'

Gleed nodded.

'A precocious child.'

'Very,' Kenworthy said.

'In the sexual sense?'

'She had that reputation and gave that impression. But then she was a child who lived on giving impressions, some of them simply capricious.'

'That's the picture that I'm left with, too. Superintendent: when Sergeant Cottier called on you this morning, you were still in bed. Your wife told him you had been up all night.'

'I couldn't sleep.'

'You suffer much from insomnia?'

'At times of stress.'

'I don't have to apologize for asking, as you know very well. But I apologize all the same: last night was a time of stress – *before* the vicar called you out?'

'Because I'd too much turning over in my mind: the play, the difficulty I was having in learning my part, the Colonel's death, whether I was bothering you people for nothing – '

Gleed had stopped taking notes.

'Yes. I've lost sleep in my time, too. But if I hadn't put the question, someone might have wanted to know why.'

CHAPTER X

Elspeth had tried not to be irritable on the journey up here. She had tried to make light of the rain, the cold, the wreck of a holiday, the incarceration in a grey cottage with once Sunshine Yellow walls. For some months before their departure for the North-West she had been struggling with mid-life, hadn't yet found the right drugs to balance the hormones. Her greatest of horrors was of becoming a bore with her symptoms; not too difficult because Simon was rarely at home. Now, with Simon involved, much of her difficulty seemed to fall away – for the time being at least. When Simon had long hours of silence, she knew how to help.

'*Nil nisi bonum,*' she said. 'That's all you can expect to hear in the village until the dust has settled. But I know, and you know, that she disgusted you. The fact that she's dead doesn't change that.'

'It does. The fact that she's dead suspends certainty. Therefore I know nothing.'

'That's because you're human as well as professional. You've always hated evil – I mean, true evil, not crime – too much for a vocational policeman.'

'In my early days, I didn't always distinguish between the two. But when I suggested she was evil, you queried it.'

'Of course I did. Don't you query every bit of evidence that comes your way? Isn't that your job?'

'But now you can come up with a firm answer?'

'Of course. How old was she? Fourteen? At that age a girl like that is capable of anything that any woman is capable of – any woman, of any age.'

'That's pitching it strong.'

'No stronger than I see it. Maturity might have taught

her more efficient techniques, but her motives were already as strong as they'd ever be. I believe what you said about her having to destroy. And once she'd confirmed what you were made of, you'd have been next on her list. There's no greater challenge than integrity. Don't let her destroy you from her present range, that's all I ask you.'

'She'll not destroy me. I have confidence in Gleed.'

'That isn't enough, Simon. In the early stages Gleed might suspect you, but that's just because he's doing his job. Clearing yourself is the least of your worries. What I mean is, don't go getting black marks for indiscretion.'

'I shall be doing nothing indiscreet. And as in my present position anything I did would be indiscreet, I propose to do nothing at all. I am at Gleed's disposal. I shall answer his questions – truthfully. I shall avoid any of the obvious associations of a guilty conscience. Above all, I shall let him see that I'm not hankering to do his work for him. He looks to me like a capable man.'

'You can afford to meet him halfway. He's not as capable a man as you are.'

A few minutes after this conversation, Dunderdale came to the cottage. It was advanced evening. Supper had been delayed by Gleed's visit. Dunderdale chose to be in hearty mood, but with shadows not far beneath the false bonhomie.

'Come along, Kenworthy. I'd hoped to find you poring over your script.'

'Script? Surely that's a thing of the past? Won't this add another year or two to the Gabbitas century?'

'Not on your life. We've just come to the end of the longest committee meeting in the history of the festival. In favour of going on with Gabbitas Week by seven votes to six.'

'You can't do it.'

'Don't say that *you'll* let us down?'

'It isn't a question of letting you down. It's a question

of what's feasible and decent. What would you do for a Gertrude?'

'Christine.'

'Christine? Horrocks's girl-friend? The one who looks like a superannuated scarecrow?'

'She did a year at RADA before opting for the communal life. John says she's good, and in that sphere even a wife wouldn't fool him. And she's not far off knowing the part. Between you and me, I think she's been the brains behind the production as it is.'

'You'll have to count me out,' Kenworthy said.

Dunderdale looked downcast, like a schoolboy, not believing in the rain on the morning of a treat.

'You can't do it,' Kenworthy said. 'With that girl having been found done to death – the whole village knowing it – '

'So we must teach them that there are limits to sentimentality. Life must go on – '

'An end put to a child's life – and you talk about sentimentality?'

'It might help you and your colleagues,' Dunderdale said. 'The opponents of Gabbitas Week may strike again. We may draw their fire.'

'No!'

Dunderdale remained crestfallen, but he was a resilient man.

'There's one other possible solution – '

'If you can find one, that's your business. Count me out. You just have to. Personal feelings apart, I can't afford any further commitment.'

'Feel like coming over to the Sergeant for a noggin?' Dunderdale asked, as if a bright change of subject neutralized any impression that he might have harboured ill-feeling.

'Are there press-men about?'

'A few.'

'I'll say no to that too, then.'

'I have a full bottle of Rémy Martin at home.'

'That does tempt me.'

He needed no second persuasion to take a look at Dunderdale's quarters. The vicarage was one of those vast old houses designed for full quivers. What bachelor needed twenty-six bedrooms? Most of them were sealed off. Dunderdale took him into a warm and welcoming study, something of a museum of his own life: intellectual – books, more about the social sciences than theology; athletics – undergraduate trophies for discus and javelin; devotional – a prie-dieu and a semi-abstract of Calvary in oils, which clearly had a real meaning in his everyday life. A guitar, too, with a small stack of beginner's albums, well thumbed: God-Rock, where Gabbitas had used Hob.

He had connoisseur's brandy glasses, and made their coffee in battered metal *filtres* that looked as if he had filched them from a boulevard.

'I must say, I had never expected you to go on with the show.'

'I am determined to foil that child, albeit posthumously. She intended to wreck it.'

'You still think so?'

'We all feel distressed about it,' Dunderdale said. 'We are bound to. But let's keep our heads and face facts.'

'Yes, let's. What facts?'

'I've been talking to some of the kids. They're all bending over backwards to speak nothing ill – especially since none of them liked her. But some of them are getting guilt complexes from what's on their minds.'

'Such as what?'

'Such as that a girl can't take a fox-terrier for a walk between school and rehearsal, and then come home without him, without someone noticing.'

'You mean she snared the animal herself and left him exposed overnight? It could fit very well. Have you told this to Gleed?'

'Not yet. I only found out this evening. I've written him a memorandum. Gleed strikes me as the kind of man it would be best to stay abreast of.'

'My opinion, too. But why should she do it? Why dish a play that was going to be the making of her name?'

'If you don't understand that, Kenworthy, then you can't have come near to understanding the girl.'

'And you did understand her?'

'We vicars were psychoanalysing centuries before Vienna invented the term.'

'She used to talk to you a lot?'

'Can't you imagine? When other ways of gaining distinction failed or palled, she could always crave audience. And let's be fair to the child, she did have problems.'

'Which had foxed the Child Guidance people?'

'Oh, you did discover that bit of her history? Do you know why they had to take her to the clinic? She'd have told you sooner or later. She couldn't keep that sort of secret for ever.'

'You tell me.'

'Because from the age of about six and a half onwards, she became obsessed with preventing her parents from having sexual intercourse.'

Kenworthy's *filtre* was clogged with grounds, and Dunderdale came to his aid with the handle of an apostle spoon.

'It started at primary school. She was taught the facts of life – biologically. What she was not taught – and I doubt whether it can be taught at that age – was the nature of passion. Her phobia arose partly out of misinformation, partly out of animal selfishness. It's three years ago that she sat where you are sitting, and told me about it in those very terms. That was her favourite weapon, a veritable bludgeon, her shattering honesty about her own wickedness. I use that word because it was her own term for it: wickedness. In her days at the junior school she connected sexual relations solely with childbirth. She thought that one must inevitably be followed by the other. And, frankly and simply, she was horrified by the thought of a rival in the family, but I think that's later rationalization. It went deeper.'

Dunderdale went through the proper motions of appreciating the bouquet of the brandy.

'She described to me very graphically the nightmares that she had at this time. But the period of misapprehension was brief. It was not long before she learned to subdue those nightmares: and to manipulate them. Of course, this was a story that she had had ample opportunity to polish in the telling. She was quick to spot what evidently gave them great satisfaction in the clinic. Her case history had to be endured by whoever happened to be her selected confessor of the moment. And she was a girl who always had to have a confessor. I cannot believe that you would have been free of the incubus much longer. But it was not absolution she wanted: it was the chance to shine. I hope this doesn't sound too much like *nil nisi malum*?'

'There is a nauseating timbre of truth about it.'

It stood out from Dunderdale's eager telling of it that there had been equal enthusiasm on both sides of the confessional.

'She staged her nightmares, beautifully timed, struggling to stay awake until her parents came upstairs, straining her ears to listen whether they went into the lavatory together. She was convinced that the lavatory was the normal place for it, because of the organs involved. This was only, I remind you, Phase One of her misunderstandings. Phase One did not last long.'

Dunderdale looked knowing. He might, for that one second, have been telling a tale in a golf club.

'Phase One did not last long – Phase Two – for the next year or so she applied herself to the study of sex, as the bright lads of your generation and mine used to apply themselves to fossils and butterflies. Some of her conversations with children of her own age, if they were ever reported at home, must have caused consternation. She had a detailed knowledge of the mechanics of contraception that left me with a feeling of callow ignorance.'

'All in a day's work, Vicar.'

'Don't get me wrong. I didn't encourage her. Once she started to talk, she went on talking.'

'One can see what split her parents up.'

'Yes; but make some allowance for their own ineptitude too. I don't think that that pair could have handled a normal child – if there is such a thing. At any rate, by the time she was eight, Davina might still not have known what love and passion meant, but she had a consummate knowledge of their outlets and inlets.'

'And they disgusted her?'

'I don't know that they disgusted her. She was obsessed by them. She must have been a horrible child. She knew what was going on behind the bedroom wall. She even knew from the looks on her parents' faces the evenings when they fancied each other. She knew the critical moment at which to sit up in bed and scream. She knew how and when to get taken into her parents' bed. She developed the sleep-walking habit – pure theatre, of course: a nine-year-old Lady Macbeth teetering on the landing. Once, and once only, she managed to break in on her mother and father in the act. And, of course, basically – here's their complete failure to cope – they were ashamed. Her father lost his temper and thrashed her. Her mother fell out with him over that – and then sheered off sex herself.'

'Which Davina knew?'

'To her smirking satisfaction. It's not easy for me to sit here and make it real for you.'

'I've had more than my share of confessional urges in my time,' Kenworthy said, 'but I've never sat it out with a child of that age on that subject.'

Dunderdale replenished their glasses. They had already made significant inroads into the bottle.

'Of course, the Stotts did not go to pieces all at once. There were attempts at a fresh start, even serious efforts to persuade the child that certain things in life are sweet and natural. She was sent away one summer to an organized children's camp, but her behaviour was outrageous, disruptive. She could not bear to be away from home, not knowing what might be going on there. She was escorted back after three days, with a strong recommendation to take her to a psychiatrist. But even then the Stotts procrastinated; still the stupidity of false shame. They did not want their social set to know that they could not manage the child. God knows what their social set did think. Davina cannot have been the most popular of guests in other people's houses – though she knew how to behave like an angel when it suited her book. If you'll excuse me a moment, I rather think a tray's been got ready for us.' Dunderdale got up suddenly. He left the room. He had revealed nothing at all about his domestic arrangements. There had to be a housekeeper in the background somewhere; the house was beautifully kept. But she had never been mentioned. Kenworthy took the chance to move inquisitively about the room. Dunderdale's current reading, over the arm of a chair, appeared to be Leggett's *First Zen Reader*. There were manuscript sheets lying about his desk that suggested that even at this late stage he was wrestling with a better ending for *The Anathema Stone*.

In a minute or two he came back, carrying a tray with a garnished board of assorted cheeses. He went on with his story as if there had been no interruption.

'The crunch came when the girl was still only ten. There had been an accident in a neighbour's house. An au-pair girl had left clips unfastened on a stair-carpet, and mother-in-law had come a cropper. Within a week

or two of that incident, Donald Stott had had to go to an
executive stag-night that came his way two or three
times a year. He usually came home late from it, flushed
and noisy – he wasn't a practised drinking man – and
Davina knew that a glass or two too many brought him
home in a randy mood. Mother had had half a bottle of
gin and betaken herself to bed early. Davina was quiet in
her bedroom, pasting pop-group cuttings into an album.
She had mastered the art of being convincingly out of
harm's way. That was the night she fixed the stair-rods.
Father had to be taken to Casualty. After that, it had to
be the clinic for her. Maybe they'd left it too late; or
maybe she was too clever for the shrinkers.'

'Full marks for this Stilton,' Kenworthy murmured.
'Local breed.'

'So the Stott family foundered? Fell out about how the
girl ought to be treated. Fell out about everything under
the sun, until they became intolerable to each other. And
Stott played the gallant, and the wife got the child.
Maybe he wasn't being all that gallant.'

'I do know that he was crippled financially,' Dunderdale said. 'And Phase Three evolved.'

'Phase Three being? Not that I don't know.'

'Onset of puberty. Sex in her own right now – aware of
her development in mirror and bath.'

'Dawning nymphomania?'

'I don't think so. I think we're going to be told by the
pathologist that she was still a virgin. I *think* so: I'm not
sure what happened one night up at the Grange. Sex still
obsessed her; but I don't think it became something she
wanted. I think it was something to wield.'

'Did you at no time think of trying to tackle the
mother?'

'You've met her. You can imagine how far I got.'

'An unofficial word with her GP?'

'Without the co-operation of either parent or child he
was powerless.'

'School?'

'I think that was her only hope. She was John Horrocks's protégée. He did more than anyone else to get her and keep her on the rails. I think she even tried to be good just to please him. And the concentration on the play this autumn has helped.'

'Other kids?'

'All scared stiff of her. She was not of their world. They knew that without understanding it.'

'So she was conscious of a new power. And who were her victims?'

But before Dunderdale could answer, there was the gentlest rap of knuckles on the study door. Dunderdale called to come in. A woman appeared, slender and well-groomed, and in her late thirties. She was wearing an outdoor coat, and did not actually come into the room.

'If that's all, Mr Dunderdale, I'll be making for home.'

'Yes, that's everything, Mrs Malkin. Thank you for the cheese.'

Malkin: the neutral clan. A Brightmore or an Allsop in the vicar's camp might have led to awkward situations. She wished them goodnight, politely and separately – but shyly, and without the presumption of a smile for either of them.

'We were talking about Davina's new power,' Kenworthy said, 'and where she was likely to try it out.'

'I hate naming names, but I must. Jesse Allsop for one, believe it or not. But nobody knows what really passed between them. For a time, as you heard this morning, she became a regular caller at Dogtooth. Then it all stopped suddenly. You saw Jesse this morning: a bachelor, tormented, a scowling introvert, commercially successful, because commercially ruthless. Perhaps that's a bit strong: commercially fierce, let's say. But tortured. Tortured by his own dark thoughts, whatever they are. Tortured by thoughts of the twisted limb of the family he's descended from. He regards himself, I think, as doomed to be an oddity, doomed to be off-beam, master of a village clan, yet doomed to be friendless.'

He interrupted himself to suggest a small piece of Cheddar for palate-cleansing.

'When a man gets into that frame of mind, he sometimes gets satisfaction by living up to the false image. You can imagine what the village children think him: a warlock; no rapport between him and them whatever. But he does use a few of them, now and then, as you heard, for work on his caravan sites. It's cheap labour, good labour at that. They're a conscientious crowd. But to Davina his inaccessibility was itself a challenge. They all thought they'd been underpaid for a piece of Bank Holiday work, and she swore she'd beard him in his den about it. She made a lone sortie to Dogtooth one evening in September last year. It was the only talking point that day amongst the Spentlow juveniles. She was gone a long time and came back with the bombshell that Jesse had invited her to tea after school the next day. Until well into the autumn Davina went regularly to Dogtooth. I might say I was unhappy about it. I kept my ear as close to the ground as I could. But that's not very close where Jesse Allsop is concerned. Then, as I say, it stopped suddenly. Nothing said. Nothing hinted.'

'You never tried to probe Allsop?'

'He simply took the line he took this morning. She kept plaguing him for non-existent arrears, and he finally gave her her marching orders.'

'I hope that Gleed will get to know all this.'

'Gleed surely knows. He was closeted with Jesse for a long time this morning. Jesse Allsop is softer than he looks. He doesn't set about it in the right way, but, more than anything else, he wants to be liked. Jesse wants it both ways. He wants to be himself, and he wants men to understand him. Davina would have the intuition and wits to keep both ends in view. Gleed may possibly overlook the need for that. You, of course, would do well with the man.'

Kenworthy made no comment on that score. Dunderdale reached again for the brandy bottle. The tide-line was now perceptibly below the halfway mark.

'Any other names to name?' Kenworthy asked.

'If you can clear your mind of prejudices against these Beaker Folk – '

'The Ultimate Anarchists?'

'You've picked up the term? A fair description of them, if by *Ultimate* you mean "never". A bunch of liberal romantics so out of tune with the existing order that they cheerfully imagine disorder to be the antidote. The advent of Davina into their midst seems to have created some major disturbance. Nobody knows what that was about, except possibly John Horrocks, and no power on earth will make him talk if he doesn't want to.'

'How deeply has he been involved with Davina?'

'Professionally. He's her teacher. And, though you may not believe it to look at him, too professional to take any risks. Apart from the fact that he's so besotted with Christine. He isn't the leader of the Folk: they don't, of course, admit to leadership. But he was a founder-member – under Christine's aegis – and, thanks to his teaching job, is the only one with roots in the ground. He is, for example, their authority on squatters' rights, and in that department his word is anarchists' law. The rest are a mixed bunch; there'll be about twenty of them when they're at full strength – there's perpetual coming and going. There is a poet or two; one man has had a sonnet accepted by a review magazine that went broke before they could print it. Another is writing a novel on an endless roll of paper. Another has had an idea for a documentary rejected by ITV in encouraging terms, and is still working on the idea. There is a potter amongst them, and if he had had a wheel he could have made them their beakers, if he had had any clay. And there was

Kevin O'Shea – '

Dunderdale paused to see what effect the name might have. Kenworthy ensured that it had none.

'Kevin O'Shea is a big stage Irishman, Mark Two. By that I mean a huge, flabby, hairy man, every square inch of his face bar his eyes sprouting untrimmed red beard. And into a gap in that beard he can insert an incredibly small and delicate tin whistle, from which he produces incredibly dextrous and delicate melody. Not the leader of the movement; I repeat, they don't have one. But the most frightening. Frightening in the eyes of the village, I mean. He really did go about looking objectionable. Noisy when drunk; usually drunk. Pugnacious in his cups; and looked pugnacious, in or out of them.'

'But you don't usually get a bunch such as this without some crime going on.'

'That's what Spentlow thinks, but I'd give the Beaker Folk a pretty clean bill. They can't traffic in drugs – they haven't the capital. For the same reason their own indulgences are modest. They don't pilfer – they are too protective of their own image. For a bunch of revolutionaries, they are an extraordinarily solemn and passive crowd. They take their ideals very seriously.'

'You see rather a lot of them, do you?'

'I have done. They fascinate me. I find them more interesting than cowmen and caravan speculators. They may be misguided, but at least they are trying.'

'And Davina saw a lot of them, too?'

'She did. She had to persevere to insinuate herself. For all their pride in their flexibility, they are an inward-looking bunch.'

'But she made it?'

'By sheer assiduity.'

'And sex?'

'I have no doubt that she was up to her usual brinkwomanship.'

'Brinkwomanship: a good word. And for the first time

in her life, she was playing round a brink that wasn't
fenced in.'

'That's just it.'

'So she might have got what she seemed to be asking
for?'

'There is a school of thought in Spentlow that believes
so. Some think she learned a memorable lesson.'

Kenworthy held two fingers over his glass at the offer
of a refill.

'Are the Beaker Folk sexually promiscuous?'

'In theory. In practice, most of the couples have stum-
bled on a natural stability.'

'So Davina, pirouetting round the edges, may have
taken too much for granted?'

'Possibly. But I don't think that that was where the
trouble lay. They believe, in the Recruiting Sergeant,
that O'Shea was responsible for the moment of truth.
She may have teased his patience without realizing that
he hadn't any. Hence my uncertainty as to whether she
was *virgo intacta*. With Kevin O'Shea as instructor it
would be a memorable lesson. He wouldn't be fingering
a dainty little flageolet this time.'

'Ought all this not to have been brought to the attention of the police or the welfare authorities?'

'On what evidence? There was none. And there was
no complaint from Davina. Whatever happened, there
wouldn't be that.'

'There ought to have been a Care and Protection
Order on the child ages ago.'

'To drive her into open rebellion against society at
large? The play was doing her far more good.'

'So what did eventually happen between her and the
Beaker Folk?'

'We don't know. We know that one night in August
Kevin O'Shea trekked away. We know that Davina
ceased to be interested in the Grange as suddenly and
completely as she had given up Jesse Allsop.'

'Gleed has plenty to work on.'

'You'd do it better than he can, Kenworthy.'

'You're very anxious to have it in my hands. It can't be, Dunderdale. I'd be the last man to want it.'

'Pity.'

Kenworthy got up and settled his glass back on the tray.

Men converged diagonally on him from the shadows as he left the vicarage.

'Is it true that the Yard have seconded you to this case, Mr Kenworthy?'

'Was it really an accident that you took a letting cottage two weeks ago, Superintendent?'

'When are you going to call a press conference, sir?'

'Can we quote you as saying that relations with the county force are all that could be desired?'

'I'm just an ordinary member of the public,' Kenworthy said, and when that failed to give any kind of satisfaction he was compelled to stand and address them.

'Do you know how many days leave a Yard man gets in a year, gentlemen? I came up to Derbyshire not to be bothered – '

They were still clamouring as he slipped through the gate. Elspeth was waiting to help him escape in through their rented front door.

CHAPTER XI

A clear day, and, for the Kenworthys, a gift island of time, like a clip from a film of what might have been. They walked miles over hilltops and across the heads of cloughs that fed ice-cold rivulets down into the dales. The air was clean. They had immense tracts of country

to themselves. Except for the white rubble walls, parcel-
ling the middle distance into tiny, irregular, unviable
fields, there was nothing on the skyline that would have
seemed alien to Neolithic man. And even the rectangular
enclosures had something about them that was primeval
in spirit.

Whatever Gleed's priorities were, he was leaving Kenworthy alone; perhaps pointedly alone. It might have
been psychological warfare; or maybe there seemed
nothing to add to the depositions that Kenworthy had
already made. There was frequent movement of police
vehicles in and out of the village. One was parked outside
the vicarage for a very long time. Sometimes the centre of
attraction was Dogtooth, and an augmented team came
and searched the farm. Diana Stott was called for and
driven to County HQ, and was away so late that it was
rumoured that she was being detained overnight. But a
car drew up outside her bungalow between eleven and
midnight, and Mrs Scadbolt reported that lights were
again showing behind the curtained windows.

Mobile teams from two rival television companies had
had to content themselves with shots of places that the
presenters tried to turn into something sinister: the Hall,
the Stotts' bungalow, the 'Roman' paving. The ubiquity
of journalists was such that Kenworthy was even done
out of his nightly beer: there were times when even 'No
Comment' could be twisted into a dangerous statement.

Just after closing time in the Sergeant, on the night
after the Kenworthys' long walk, there was a knock on
the door, which Elspeth answered. John Horrocks was
standing there, courteous, and strangely unsure of himself. Kenworthy came to him.

'Mr Kenworthy – I wonder if I could trespass on your
time and goodwill. I'd like to ask your professional
advice.'

'By all means. Come in.'

Kenworthy caught sight of the pale, motionless and amorphous figure that was Christine. She had not entered the gate.

'We won't, if you don't mind. I was wondering if you would be so kind as to come back with us to the Grange. That is – I know it's a tricky business, asking the opinion of an off-duty policeman – '

'You can at least try me out.'

'I mean – nobody knows for certain whether you *are* off duty.'

There was still something untypically nervous about him.

'That seems to be everyone's problem. Let's put it this way: I am off duty, but being careful, very careful. In any case, if it's advice you want, I don't think I'd be very good at talking to an Ultimate Anarchist about the law.'

John Horrocks laughed, after a fashion, but the pleasantry had not been enough to put him at his ease. There was no response at all from Christine.

'You mustn't get us wrong, Mr Kenworthy. Ultimate Anarchy acknowledges that the world is not yet ready for ideal lawlessness. What we believe and practise among ourselves is not something to be forced on others.'

'I'm relieved to hear it. What's your problem?'

'I'd prefer to leave that, if you don't mind. It's a decision that faces our community as a whole. If they think I've briefed you in advance, then both you and I will be rejected.'

Elspeth was already holding Kenworthy's coat for him. He and Horrocks joined Christine on the pavement. She moved round so that Horrocks was in the middle; but it was the proximity of Kenworthy that she was trying to avoid.

They walked together up the hill towards the Grange – a long mile, and a steep road that they eventually left to follow a drive between dilapidated lodge gates. Spentlow Grange was a late nineteenth-century parvenu creation that had fallen into disuse out of economic impossibility: any owner who could have afforded to keep it up could have laid out his money on something significantly more comfortable. The trio moved under dark trees, a dank fungoid smell rising from the undergrowth. Before they came in sight of the lights of the house, they heard the sound of decidedly amateur flamenco guitar. There had been virtually no conversation on the way up, attempts at inconsequentiality petering out as artificial. As they were approaching the front door – one glass panel replaced by the side of a cardboard carton, another by a sheet of sacking – Horrocks was constrained to make yet another apologetic preamble.

'I hope, Mr Kenworthy, that you won't judge irretrievably by your first impressions.'

'I hope I'm not coming to judge at all.'

'But you're bound to, aren't you? I mean, your world – '

'Do you mean my bourgeois ghetto – or my fascist bacon-factory?'

'What I mean is – you're about to come up against prejudice.'

'And you're afraid I can't stand up for myself?'

The bare wooden floor of the entrance hall had been swept, but if it had been scrubbed when they first took up occupation, no sort of job had been made of it. The grime had merely been swirled about and left to dry. Ethical enlightenment went hand in hand with either physical inertia or circumstantial purblindness. Moreover, there was a smell of recently-burned joss-sticks, and Kenworthy knew what that was probably meant to screen.

Horrocks showed him into a ground-floor room at the front of the house, where a number of people were gathered in knots in an incomplete circle. The windows were uncurtained, the furniture was rudimentary. There were cushions on the floor, an old mattress or two, even the frame of a rucksack serving as a sort of armchair.

There seemed to be about a dozen men and women present, in all manner of costume, drabness prevailing. Even their patchwork skirts and their sweaters bedecked with cheap badges and escutcheons seemed singularly colourless. Horrocks looked round, making a mental roll-call.

'Someone go and fetch Bob and Catherine. I want a full house.'

A messenger went, and a tall girl in a sleeveless black H-line dress got up and made for the door.

'Triss, I want you to stay.'

'*You* want me to stay?'

'*We* want you to stay.'

'But I know what we're going to hear.'

'In that case, you might affect the majority decision.'

'I don't believe in majority decisions. They coerce the minority. Everything worthwhile in history has been achieved by minorities.'

'Then stay and achieve something now.'

'I shall only become insulting.'

'Mr Kenworthy can stand that.'

'*Mister* Kenworthy!'

Horrocks looked round the room for support. Most of those present were putting on an act of aggressive boredom.

'We are going to make a decision tonight – after we have heard all points of view. If we do not hear all points of view, the decision will be a false one.'

Christine came forward, grasped the tall girl by the shoulders and pushed her back towards the nest of gutless cushions from which she had risen. At the same time, the couple who must be Bob and Catherine came in: a man with a head of hair like a Kaffir, and a girl with a baby at her bared breast.

'I do not propose to act as chairman,' Horrocks began.

'We do not have chairmen,' Triss said. 'A chairman can only inhibit.'

'Therefore my role is solely that of Prologue. We are here because a girl has been murdered.'

'Whereat all subscribers to conventional religions should surely rejoice. Because they believe she has gone – '

'I object,' a man said, 'to this quest for advice from an acknowledged authoritarian.'

'Authoritarians are, alas, what we are going to be up against in the very near future. Uncompromising authoritarians. It is because of that that we owe it to ourselves to hear the legalist viewpoint. The threat to this community, my friends, is very great.'

Horrocks was trying to be persuasive with dignity; but dignity was itself suspect in this circle.

'We are not going to promise ourselves that we will do what Mr Kenworthy advises. But we would be fools not to hear his advice.'

'But why, for God's sake? We didn't murder the girl!'

'No. But as a community, we know we have something on our conscience.'

'Conscience is only a manifestation of social conditioning,' someone said.

'I'll put it a different way, then. There is not one member here who is not *ashamed* – '

'Shame is only – '

'Oh, shut up, Triss.'

The man who protested was a lumbering specimen wearing spectacles in round tortoiseshell frames that must date back to the 1920s.

'What was done was not done in the name of the community.'

'It was done by a substantial number of us.'

'It was not. Why fight shy of the facts? It was done by a handful of women.'

There was a ripple of female dissent.

'I fail to see what that incident has to do with the murder of the girl.'

'It hasn't – '

'It has,' – this was the man in the spectacles again – 'if the girl had been treated according to the principles on which we pride ourselves – '

'I don't know why this has been brought up, anyway.'

'It has been brought up,' Horrocks said, 'because it's only a matter of time before it's brought up by someone who's going to be neither patient nor tolerant. It's not the sort of thing that can be kept dark. It *hasn't* been kept dark. Keeping it dark might even make it seem worse than it was.'

'So what's your proposition, then, John? That someone volunteers to go and tell them the truth?'

'That we first establish what the truth was.'

'Casuistry. You mean, cook it? Concoct an agreed version?'

'No. Establish the true version.'

'So you bring in one of the Elder Brethren,' a man said, 'to hear us argue it out? Hoping that he'll leak it back and salve your tender conscience that way? I'm sorry,' he said sideways to Kenworthy. 'I'm quite sure that you're the nicest of chaps. I would be delighted to go with you on a walking tour of the Vosges. But you do happen to be our enemy.'

Kenworthy stood up.

'Thank you. I dare say you're quite a reasonable sort of cove yourself, though I'll pass up on your holiday offer, if you don't mind. I'm sorry if I seem to have been brought here to try to force a premature decision. But it does seem to me that you're sitting on something pretty uncomfortable. And it's also plain that you're not ready to agree any statement yet. I can't think that my presence is anything but a hindrance. If John Horrocks can find me somewhere private to sit it out – '

'Privacy is several kinds of theft,' Triss said. She was ignored.

Horrocks took him upstairs to what he called the

Quiet Room, a sort of communal study with bookcases improvised from the ubiquitous cardboard cartons.

'I hope you don't think I brought you here just to force their hands.'

'That's what I do think, as a matter of fact. And a damned good idea, too, if I may say so.'

'Something happened here last summer. Something involving Davina and Kevin O'Shea. I've a rough idea what, but the details are elusive. It may be irrelevant to the final issue, but if your colleagues find out about it before we tell them ourselves it's going to complicate matters no end.'

Left alone, Kenworthy looked over their library. It was obvious that the books had been pooled from three or four major sources: there was exotic religion – Zoroastrianism and the Occult; Pelican sociology; Marxist economics. On a rough deal table Horrocks had been correcting school exercise books – apparently with great pains. He caught sight of a dog-eared copy of *The Anathema Stone* script. He picked it up and lifted the weather-stained top sheet. The stapling had come undone and a few of the lower sheets were missing. He recognized alterations to stage directions in Davina's hand. She had had this copy with her the morning they had been saddled with Mrs Scadbolt. She had also had it that last night when he had said goodnight to her outside her bungalow. How could it have got there, unless she had brought it herself?

He picked up a book: Zimmermann's *Vademecum for Activists*: time-pencils, self-igniting phosphorus bottles, subversion by blackmail, infiltration of media. He read one chapter at length: *How to make friends with the enemy*.

Then, footsteps up the uncarpeted stairs; a strangely dragging gait: Christine in a long, shapeless dress, in some material that had once been white, her sandals loose about her heels. She came and stood framed in the open door, looked at him, took note of what he was

reading, her face as accusing as her expressionless eyes
could be. Of all the Beaker Folk he had met, she was the
one who remained implacably hostile.

'They want you downstairs.'

A lazy voice, as if even the passing of this message to
him was something for which she prayed cosmic forgive-
ness. He stood up, and she swung round with her back to
him to lead him downstairs.

'How does this come to be here?'

'That?'

'No. Not Zimmermann. That can be bought over the
counter, more's the pity. But it doesn't worry me – it
takes staying-power to be a terrorist – more than you've
got in this bunch. No: I mean this – Davina Stott's
script.'

She seemed to come near to a moment of pleasure: no
more than a movement of her upper lip; but it was a
tremor of satisfied contempt.

'The vicar. He returned it to John.'

He began to follow her down the stairs, keeping his
distance, because she was having as much difficulty with
the long dress as with the sandals. She might at least
have held it up about her ankles, but gave the impression
that she rejected anything so ladylike. She seemed to
prefer to risk breaking her neck through the hem
catching under her toes and heels.

But not for long. They had not gone far down the stairs
when the hall below them was suddenly full of noise, of
feet and men's voices. Two uniformed constables rushed
past them up the stairs, ordering them down to join the
others in the common room on the ground floor. Boots
clattered up to the landing above them: the stock tactics
for shock house search – the advance party rushing up to
the top of the building whilst bewilderment lasted; the
remote corners occupied whilst the argument over war-
rants was still going on with the principals.

Gleed was down there, holding the stage in their

common room. Kenworthy also recognized Sergeant
Cottier. And on the edge of the headquarters party was
Bill Clingo, evidently on secondment.

'I want everyone to stand by his own possessions.'

'We don't have possessions.'

That was the girl Triss, her laughter tinkling and
provocative.

'Then you, you and you will come with us. The rest of
you stay here.'

Gleed thus nominated his prospective witnesses,
among them Horrocks and the man with the Kaffir hair;
but not including Christine. Her anger at being omitted
seemed even greater than her indignation at the fact of
the raid; her face drained of what vestiges of colour it had
had. Kenworthy tried to catch Gleed's eye; but Gleed
wasn't playing. Bill Clingo nodded to him in such a way
as to discourage contact. Clearly Bill was under injunction, and not scripted to say anything yet. A uniformed
man misinterpreted Kenworthy's apartness from the
group.

'Go in there with the rest of them. Don't let's have any
trouble.'

CHAPTER XII

The raid and house search of the Beaker Folk's quarters
took all of two and a half hours, for the whole of which
time Kenworthy had to sit under the eye of a passively
pugnacious looking constable, alongside the small-fry of
the community. Unreason was sweet to these people at
the lower end of the anarchical pecking order, and they
dropped easily into the assumption that Kenworthy's
visit had had something to do with the mounting of this
invasion. They sat in boredom, frustrated in their efforts
to interpret the noisy feet in adjacent rooms. Many of

these were empty, but it sounded as if every loose floor-board, and a good many sound ones, were being investi-gated. Once, a child started howling, and a woman was allowed upstairs to attend to it. Once, a small party came down into the hall with such purposeful clattering that it sounded as if a critical juncture had been reached. But nothing came of it, and it was after two a.m. that the maddeningly leisurely process was wound up. It then became obvious that one man, one woman and John Horrocks were going to accompany Gleed back to his headquarters. Only then did Kenworthy have the chance to sidetrack Bill Clingo. Clingo, with the reputa-tion of a rustic – largely on account of a sing-song accent which it had never occurred to him to lose – had trans-ferred to the Met. from the East Anglian force in the early 1950s. He was a good copper, with a gluttonous capacity for work, but also with a collector's appetite for his personal records: a small-minded man. As a result, he went for small profits and quick returns, and was something of a joke at the Yard for his rounding-up of lesser lights. Perhaps that was why he was one of the oldest inspectors on the ground: he suffered from an unaffected satisfaction with his own achievements.

And so it had been again now. Kenworthy could see that Clingo was puffed with the feeling of having pulled something off. And he could not conceal his feeling that his own standing was good locally, while Kenworthy was clearly out in the shade.

'Thanks for the tip-off, Simon.'

'Did you a bit of good, did it?'

'We picked up O'Shea in Nuneaton yesterday.'

'On what sort of rap?'

Clingo's pleasure knew no bounds. He did not nor-mally work anywhere near Kenworthy. His deference for rank was within a shade of immaculacy. But what was not immaculate about it was the way his self-satisfaction showed through.

'You mean you don't know? For heaven's sake don't tell Gleed that I've told you – '

Kenworthy maintained both his patience and his patient appearance.

'Illegal immigrants.'

'You mean they've been using this place as a transit camp?'

'That's the object of the present exercise.'

'I was under the impression that it had to do with the death of a girl.'

'That first and foremost, but between you and me, there's a lot on the side.'

Then Gleed came up to them, and Clingo all but jumped nervously. Yet the Derbyshire Chief Inspector looked in no way betrayed at seeing him talking to Kenworthy. He nodded as if they were his familiar spirits.

'You've finished with me?' Kenworthy asked.

'Of course. You'd have been free to go a couple of hours ago, if I'd spotted how you were being treated.'

Kenworthy managed to look as if he believed that. There were a couple of minutes of headlamp confusion as police vehicles shunted themselves away from the Grange. As Kenworthy was leaving down the front steps he met Christine coming back into the house, apparently having tried to take some sort of leave of Horrocks as he was driven away. Somehow she combined raging dignity with a stance contemptuously devoid of all grace. A curtain of hair hung in front of her eyes. It was surprising that she could see anything at all.

'Satisfied, Kenworthy?'

He stood and looked at her silently, so that she did not know whether he was about to lose his temper, or reason with her smoothly, or start to question her, or perhaps insult her with a phrase or two of hypocritical small talk. He stood thus for the space of half a dozen leisurely breaths, then turned away into the night without saying anything.

The unshaded, uncurtained lights of the Grange receded behind him. He was engulfed in the avenue shadows of the drive as if at the whim of a stage electrician's dimmer. It was a warmer night than any the Kenworthys had had since the dislocated prop-shaft had knocked hell out of its cross-members. It was warm, unrelievedly dark, and damp-feeling still, though it had not actually rained for two days. He came out into the open road by the ruined lodge, relieved to escape from the heavy fungoid smell. Spentlow lay a mile or so below him, its lights, if any were still burning, concealed by the lie of the trees and the hair-pins of the road. On a distant hill-flank a dog was howling, disconsolate and ignored. Nearer at hand he heard the unavailing shriek of some vole taken by an owl. Otherwise there was no sound other than the air among fallen leaves, in itself a kind of silence.

Until, that is, he was within twenty yards of the last bend, which would bring him down over the lip of the village bowl. It was here that he first heard the engine of a vehicle coming up out of Spentlow: a heavy engine, one that had suffered much abuse in its time, the exhaust perforated, the throttle wide open to match its task. And now headlamps were striking up through the trees, spreading a fan of unidentifiable shadows. Kenworthy edged into the wall, thinking that the thing would be rounding the narrow bend and upon him before the driver saw him. But before it reached the corner the vehicle turned. There was a change of engine tone after the unskilful engagement of a lower gear, the struggle of wheels as they sought to grip an inimical surface, the splintering of wood as something was struck. Kenworthy hurried down to the corner, but could not make out what was happening, except that the thing had turned off the road up a field track, and was making heavy weather of a steep gradient and a glutinous surface. From its close-set beams he put it down as a Land-Rover or some such.

He might, then, have let it go at that, had it not become apparent that the driver was getting into more, and unusual, difficulty. The engine stalled, and needed several touches of the starter. There was again the whine of skidding wheels, this time on muddy grass. Kenworthy was now abreast of the field gate into which it had turned, and examined by torchlight the wrecked post whose splintering he had heard. By now the driver was coasting some yards downhill in reverse in order to find himself an easier slope for a fresh take-off. The lights slewed round, playing now laterally across a rough hillside dotted with sparse shrubs and ribbed with sheepridges. The vehicle started forward again; but the manoeuvre failed badly. Kenworthy was now near enough to pick up a tractor in his torchbeam, and to see that it was drawing a two-wheeled trailer. It was an ancient tractor, perhaps even an historic model, without hood or any kind of protective superstructure. And, as Kenworthy's beam found it, it lurched over to its right, lost equilibrium on the uneven terrain, and began to totter sideways, dragging the trailer off its wheels behind it. In the same moment the driver had the presence of mind to throw himself off the seat to his left.

The assemblage did not fall far, but was brought up short by the furrows that it had ploughed. There was the sound of more woodwork breaking, the smell of escaping petrol, and Kenworthy raced uphill towards the man, who had flung himself clear. Already he was pulling himself to his feet, cursing loudly, and then, when he saw the newcomer, berating him as an intruder.

'Who are you and what are you doing in this field? You know you are trespassing?'

Jesse Allsop: Jesse Allsop with a huge load of drink in him, though it was hard to see how incompetently drunk he was. He was too drunk to drive the ancient tractor that he had not handled for years – yet not too drunk to make some effort at pulling himself together when Ken-

worthy made himself known. All the same, his first
instinct was to get down to the capsized trailer and get
some idea as to how extricable the situation was.

'One thing's obvious,' Kenworthy said. 'You're not
going to be able to retrieve that tonight. Or get breakdown equipment within striking distance until the
ground has dried out.'

For the moment, Allsop was more taken up with the
state of the trailer than he was in volunteering explanations. The thing had turned full turtle and was obscuring
whatever load it had carried.

'Not a bloody hope,' Allsop said, more to himself than
to Kenworthy. 'It's under a curse to the last yard home.'

Kenworthy understood that 'it' was the Stone.

'Trying to take it back where it came from, were you?'

'It should never have been brought down in the first
place. And that wasn't my doing. Two and a half centuries before my time. But somebody has to put things
back to rights. Has to bloody well try, anyway.'

An intelligent, commercially competent man, convinced that he could assuage an ancient evil by returning
a slab of carboniferous lime to the spot chosen for it four
millennia ago? Somehow, on that benighted hillside,
with the tractor's headlights still carving uncouth angles
through the long grass, there seemed almost an element
of logic behind it. Allsop went to the tractor and tried to
get an arm to the dashboard under the smashed steering
column.

'What are you trying to do?'

'Switch off. The battery will be flat in no time.'

'If ever you get this back down to the road, you'll have
bigger things to worry about than the battery.'

'I can't leave the lamps burning all night.'

'Why not?'

'They'll be seen. Everybody will know.'

'Does that matter? Won't they all know, come the
dawn? You'd be better off in the warmth and comfort of

Dogtooth, making us both a cup of strong, black coffee.'

'Warmth? Comfort? Dogtooth? You've never lived there.'

'If I did, the place would be what I cared to make of it. I wouldn't let myself be buggered about by a half-baked legend.'

'You can talk like that. You'll be back in London the week after next.'

A flash of impeccable clarity.

'How about that coffee, Jesse?'

'They're thinking now that I killed the girl,' Allsop said, his brain working in compulsive jerks.

'Let's go down to your place and talk about that.'

On their way across the yard it was obvious that the offending doorstep had been rooted out by savage force.

'Billy Malkin and one or two of them gave me a hand with it. We got it on the trailer with block and tackle. But not one of them would come with me the rest of the way. We could have got it back where it belongs between us.'

Kenworthy said nothing until the coffee was made and Allsop had brought it into the living-room. His load of drink was wearing thin now but he was showing the combined effects of shock, fatigue and overall confusion. He was not wearing his worn, sober suit tonight, but a jumble of working clothes suitable to the job he had been doing. His hair, however, had clearly been sleekly combed when he set out.

'I don't understand a hard-headed man like yourself getting into this kind of state over a story.'

'You haven't lived with it all these years, Mr Kenworthy. There'd be a curse on the Allsops, that's what the man said, more than a couple of hundred years ago.'

'I suppose a man can reach the stage where he isn't going to take chances on it.'

'I blame the vicar,' Allsop said. 'It's that Dunderdale who won't let the thing die, keeping on about history, reminding people of things better forgotten. He still keeps on about a piece of land I wouldn't sell them just after the war, for children's swings and see-saws. I bet he's put it in his silly new fairy-tale book. Why should I sell it to them at their price? They've all chosen to stay in dairy herds and what they can get from the Milk Marketing Board. I've gone for land and the holiday traffic. It's my living. Why should I give it away? They don't give me their cows.'

Gertrude Allsop looked down at them from her portrait; dull eyes, yet uncompromisingly demanding.

'That's what I mean, Jesse. You're a successful man. The most successful man in this village. The only one who knows what he wants to do with himself, and goes to it in a straight line. And from what I've picked up of local history, that went for your father and grandparents before you. That doesn't sound to me like having a curse on you.'

'You don't know, Mr Kenworthy. Now there's *this* – '

This meant everything, coming to a climax in the last interview he had had with Gleed. Kenworthy waited, looking closely at Allsop, a miserable man, misery pushed to the last tether of sanity.

'Why did it have to happen on *my* doorstep? On *that* stone?'

'Perhaps someone's been trying to get at you.'

'I don't know about that. I know I've no friends, and I don't know why that should be. I've done tight deals in my time, but never anything that wasn't fair. Never anything to make me that kind of enemy. I know I may have made mistakes in my time – '

'Such as what?'

'When they took me to court, some of them, the preservation people, to try to make me put the stone back. I stuck to my rights – if only because right *is* right. The judge was on my side. He said that when it all happened the stone belonged to an Allsop. It was his to do what he liked with. I won through. I was right. But I know now that in a way I was wrong. That's when I ought to have put the stone back.'

'Maybe. But a court hearing like that doesn't make people kill young girls and plant them on other people's doorsteps.'

'That's what's happened, Mr Kenworthy.'

'I know. And we can rely on Chief Inspector Gleed to find out how and why. It won't be for the reason you think. It won't be because of any curse on your family. Because you and I, Jesse Allsop, are hard-boiled men with a sound knowledge of the concrete things about us. You know a cow from a caravan, and I know a hobgoblin from a murderer. But if a man were to *believe* that he had a curse on him, then things might be different. A curse that exists in the imagination can be every bit as fearsome as the real thing. But there's only one curse of which I see any evidence in your life.'

Allsop's eyes now looked as Davina's dog's had in the trap. Kenworthy gave him a few seconds in which to fail to think of an answer.

'It's a curse you could do something about yourself, if you would. Only it seems to me that you prefer to accept things as they are.'

'I don't know what you mean, Mr Kenworthy.'

'I'm talking about the curse of loneliness, Jesse.'

The dart struck home. Allsop's expression was all self-pity.

'But there was one little period, not very long ago, when you thought you'd found the answer to it, didn't you? You found that somebody liked you. I want you to tell me about how Davina started coming here.'

'I've told all that to Mr Gleed.'

'But I'm looking at it from a different angle.'

'She came here the first time, as I told you when Mr Dunderdale was here. She said there was a mistake in the wages book. I showed her there wasn't, and she saw that.

But she stayed on to talk afterwards, and she wasn't like
the other kids. A man could talk to her.'

'About what sort of thing?'

'About everything. History, and prehistoric burial-
grounds, and television. And why people like to come for
holidays here.'

'So you asked her to tea the next day?'

Davina Stott, assuaging Jesse Allsop's solitude – but
only for the sake of the figure she cut in the eyes of those
she wanted to impress –

'I did. And she came often enough in the next few
weeks, of her own accord.'

'And she told you a lot about herself?'

'A lot.'

'Such as what?'

'Such as what she'd been like as a child. How she used
to plague her parents.'

'And I must ask you this – I must have a true answer –
was there ever anything between you except talk?'

'I can only say what I said to Mr Gleed; nothing happened.'

'And how hard did she try to make something
happen?'

'She didn't try at all.'

'No? My impression is that she did so with every other
male she encountered. She wasn't far off trying it on with
me.'

'I'll swear on my honour that I neither touched her,
nor thought of doing so.'

'But did she touch you?'

'Anyone can see that you and Gleed come from the
same stable. Yes; she touched me. She put her hand on
mine and left it there.'

'And you liked that?'

'Mr Kenworthy – a girl lays her hand on a man's
knuckles. That doesn't make him guilty of indecent
assault.'

'Did she ever talk to you about intimate matters?'

Like the prostitute who keeps the pack of obscene photographs for the client who needs rousing; some men can be roused by talking to them about things that they think are taboo.

'I'm telling you the truth, Mr Kenworthy. There were times when she tried to.'

'About what kind of thing, Jesse?'

'About birth control, and sex before marriage, and free love, and that sort of thing.'

'You discussed all this with her freely?'

'No, I wouldn't discuss such things at all. I always headed her off.'

'Why do that?'

'Because I am an old-fashioned man, Mr Kenworthy. I understand that the young generation have a freedom about these things quite different from ours, and that is probably a good thing. But it still goes against the grain with me.'

'Is that the only reason?'

'What other reason could there be?'

'Because she disturbed you, Jesse. We are a couple of normal men, you and I, and you know very well what I mean by "disturb you". Did she disturb you?'

'No. Because I always scotched it when things started turning that way.'

'But it is true that you could have been disturbed. Jesse: in my book there are circumstances in which a man isn't to be blamed if certain things happen.'

'Nothing did happen, Mr Kenworthy. I was determined it shouldn't.'

'So that is why, in the end, you stopped her from coming?'

'I didn't stop her from coming. She stopped herself. And even that isn't the real truth, in my opinion. She was stopped.'

'Stopped? By whom?'

'If I could answer that, perhaps you and Gleed could go home.'

Kenworthy seemed to think that there was little more to be wheedled out of Allsop on that score.

'At any rate,' he said, as he finally took his leave, 'maybe things will clear themselves up soon. We'll see if you have made things any better by getting rid of the Anathema Stone.'

'I'm not rid of it, Mr Kenworthy. It still lies in one of my fields.'

CHAPTER XIII

The detainees from Spentlow Grange were returned to their quarters before nine o'clock next morning. Bob Foster, the one with the Kaffir mop, and Patricia Cave, known by preference as Triss, had been charged with possession of a small quantity of cannabis resin. No charge had been preferred against John Horrocks. They were driven back to the derelict house in a police car, with whose driver all three of them seemed to have established friendly terms. It was understood that the local authority was setting machinery in motion to secure the eviction of the Beaker Folk.

This news was brought authoritatively to the Kenworthy household by Mrs Scadbolt, whose confident reporting was in no way embarrassed by the speed with which the information seemed to have reached her. Nor was her knowledge supported by such scholarly apparatus as acknowledgement of sources; yet ultimate confirmation proved her to have been reasonably accurate.

Kenworthy was not up early enough to receive the situation report at first hand. Elspeth had left him to sleep off naturally the activities of the night, and it was half past ten before he was up. He was still breakfasting, in negligent rather than merely casual costume, when Chief Inspector Gleed drew up outside.

Courteous, his head clearly filled with nothing but business, Gleed was nevertheless off-puttingly distant when Kenworthy stressed his readiness to help.

'Actually, I would greatly prefer it if you would come along with me to headquarters.'

'The last time I said that to a man, Gleed, it had sinister significance. Well, of course; I don't mind. You want to play me away from home? You shall.'

During the three-quarter-hour journey from the bleaker hill country down to an arterial road, Gleed apparently saw the need for conversation – a flowing yet shallow conversation about the changing economic structure of the region. The conversation long-circuited itself self-consciously away from Davina Stott and the Beaker Folk. Kenworthy made no effort to plunge them into more pressing matters.

He was left alone for upwards of twenty minutes in an ordinary interview room, perhaps even the same one in which Horrocks and company had been questioned. Gleed disappeared for a while; it might have been a stage in his psychological preparations, it might be that he had come back to his office to find his attention suddenly demanded in all directions. The HQ must suffer chronically from shortage of space and corners for privacy. When Gleed finally returned he was carrying a neat folder that had Kenworthy's name on it followed by a complex index number.

'Mr Kenworthy, my colleagues and I have greatly appreciated the care you have taken not to get under our feet. For our part, we have done our best to respect the fact that you are on holiday.'

He said this as if he had learned the speech by heart; a man who did not need to learn his speeches by heart.

'Your initial statements and the various memoranda you have submitted are full and clear. They pose virtually no demands for further clarification, except here and there for some detail that is no doubt due to slow perception on our part. All you have told us accords closely with the evidence of other witnesses. All of which, of course, is no more than we would expect from you.'

Gleed pushed the file away from himself so that it lay on the table midway between them.

'The time is overdue when I would welcome your comments on some aspects of the case that may not have occurred to you.'

The file was pushed another few inches along the standard issue yellow beechwood table.

'I want to stress, Mr Kenworthy, that this is not a file *on* you. It is a file *for* you – to put you in the picture.'

It looked, from a glance at the first item, as if it were indeed the sort of dossier prepared to brief an officer new to the case. A lot of clerical care had gone into it.

The first sheet was an abstract from the pathologist's report, shorn of its detail, even of much that might have been of secondary significance. Its principal certainty was that the immediate cause of death had been collapse of the pharynx; that bruising about the throat and at the back of the neck suggested prolonged digital pressure by a strong and medium-sized hand. Depressions in the flesh of the body suggested that it had been manhandled over a long distance, with frequent changes of grip. It seemed likely, but was not certain, that at least two persons had been involved in this transportation: there were faint marks suggesting that heels and ankles had been handled, as well as other parts of the body; but the main effort had been applied under the armpits, and there were abrasions about the lower legs and feet suggestive of their having been dragged a considerable way over rough ground. It was emphasized, however, that the only conclusion that could be categorically maintained was the original cause of death.

Kenworthy grunted with the satisfaction of a man to whom supposedly fundamental revelations come as no surprise. He turned to the second item.

Extract from statement by Vera Scadbolt, née Brightmore, married woman, part-time household help to Mr and Mrs S. Kenworthy.

On Thursday, 12th October, I met Mrs Kenworthy in the Spar Grocery Store, Spentlow, and she told me that because of the work she was doing for the amateur theatricals, sewing and so forth, she had changed her mind about employing me at her rented cottage. I therefore reported for work at about a quarter to ten, to find Mr Kenworthy alone in the house, his wife having gone to Derby to buy make-up for the actors. Mr Kenworthy seemed preoccupied, and I cannot say that he was overjoyed to see me. When I had been there about twenty minutes Davina Stott arrived, and I could see that he had obviously been expecting her. They sat very close together on the settee with her shoulder nuzzled up against his, and I said to myself, 'Vera, that isn't the first time they have sat like that.' They talked about working together to help Mr Kenworthy to learn his part, and I heard one of them say, I cannot be certain which, that it would be a good idea for them to go for long walks together, reciting their speeches.

After this conversation had gone on for some time Mr Kenworthy came to the sink to fill the kettle to make coffee. I could see that I was not wanted there by either of them, and it was at this stage that Mr Kenworthy asked me to leave the room and go and work upstairs. When he said this the girl laughed in what I can only describe as an unpleasant manner. Well, a dirty laugh would be the right word for it.

When I went upstairs I must accidentally have left the door open, because I could hear them talking together in low voices. I could not hear what they were talking about, but when I came down to empty rubbish in the yard they started talking much more loudly, and I was sure that they had changed the subject for my benefit. They were talking about the play again now, and then went on about the country walks they were going to have.

Mrs Kenworthy came back at about half past twelve and I could tell from her tone that she was put out to find the girl in the house. Davina made excuses and said that she had only come here to talk about the play.

The next evening, that would be Friday, I was taking my dog out to do his duty when I happened to run into Mrs Geraldine Cartwright, who had been over at the Hall, and we talked for a few minutes while I was waiting for Nelson to make up his mind to perform. We happened to come past the Kenworthys' cottage and I could hear their voices. I think they were talking in bed. There seemed to be some sort of quarrel going on. I heard Mrs Kenworthy tell her husband that the girl had a crush on him and that a man of his age ought to know better than to encourage her.

The second statement was corroborative evidence from Mrs Cartwright.

My name is Geraldine Cartwright and I first met Mr Kenworthy when he came into the Village Hall about a week ago. I do not know why he had come in, curiosity I think, but seeing him at a loose end I asked him if he would stand in at rehearsal for Colonel Noakes, who had failed to appear. He acted a scene with the vicar, and then one with Davina Stott. It was a scene of amusing intimacies, at a low level of comedy, and they both thoroughly enjoyed themselves. The producer had to tell them not be too realistic about it. They got on well together at rehearsals, and when not required on stage would often sit apart from the rest of the cast on the edge of the Boys' Club vaulting-horse. On such occasions they always seemed to be talking intensely, and sometimes had to be reminded that they had missed a cue to make an entrance. I do not know what they were talking about.

On the night that the poor girl was killed I had been at the Hall, and was late helping to finish some curtains, when I ran into Mrs Vera Scadbolt, who was exercising her dog. We exchanged a few words and chanced to pass the cottage that the Kenworthys have rented. It is not my habit to listen in to other people's conversations, but I could not help overhearing this one, as their voices were raised. Mrs Kenworthy was annoyed with her husband over the way he had walked with the girl across the Green after that night's rehearsal. She said that they were like a couple of lovers out of Thomas Hardy, and she quoted a line of poetry to him. I cannot now remember what it was.

Extract from statement by Mrs Doreen Malkin, housekeeper, Spentlow.

On Friday, 13th October, I had gone over to the Village Hall to carry a message to Mr Dunderdale, and I stayed on to watch some of the rehearsal. Afterwards I saw Mr Kenworthy set off with Davina Stott across the Green. I heard him say to her, 'I will walk you home.' She did not seem very keen on this at first, but then he said he had not been able to make much progress with her under the eagle eye of Mrs Scadbolt. Then they both laughed and she took his arm and rested her head against his shoulder. They went off together.

Extract from statement by Alfred Malkin Allsop, milk roundsman, Spentlow.

Last Friday night, between ten and half past, I went to the Spentlow Village Hall, to meet my girl-friend, Lorraine Scadbolt, who had been practising for a crowd scene in the vicar's play. As we were crossing the Green together, we passed a couple in the dark and I recognized the two voices as Davina Stott and the London detective Kenworthy. I could not hear all they were saying, but it was something about not getting on very well with physical contacts, and I thought to myself, 'Oy! Oy! Well, you're in the right company to learn a few lessons tonight, brother.' And then I think they must have known there was somebody else about, because they started talking loudly, something about a hat-stand in Scarborough, and cracking on they were still practising part of the play.

Extract from statement by Alice Everett Brightmore, married woman, Spentlow.

At about half past nine on Friday last I went down to Colonel Noakes's cottage to see to his Labrador. There was no arrangement that I should do this, but I normally look in three days a week to help to keep the place tidy for him, and I thought that somebody ought to be looking after the animal. I was coming out of the lane, towards the Green, as people were breaking up from the Hall, and two people passed me on their way down to Sidi Barrani. I recognized Davina Stott's voice but did not know the man, though I now suppose it to have been the London detective Kenworthy. He asked her how she had liked playing the love scenes with Colonel Noakes, and she said she much preferred playing them with him.

*Extract from aide-memoire of conversation between Chief
Inspector M. Gleed and Mrs E. Kenworthy, Monday 16th
October.*

(N.B. This is not a voluntary statement, is not
guaranteed to be an accurate record of the dialogue
and has been recorded and included purely as a personal mnemonic)

Q: You weren't seriously concerned about your
husband's relationship with this child, were you?

A: No, not seriously concerned. He's a wise and
experienced man.

Q: But all the same you did not want him to get too
closely involved?

A: He knew better than to get himself involved, but
I do know that a man, any man, can be flattered by an
attractive girl who appears to be singling him out for
attention.

Q: And she *was* singling him out?

A: It was the way they were thrown together in this
silly play. And they talk about a man being at a
dangerous age, don't they? Don't get me wrong: I've
never had the slightest reason to be worried about
Simon. But I've never supposed he's fundamentally
different from any other man. What I'm trying to say
is, I'd trust him in the *Arabian Nights*, but I'd have
better peace of mind if he weren't there. It isn't a question of trust. It's all tied up with position and dis-
cretion.

Q: You thought he was being indiscreet with
Davina Stott?

A: Not actually indiscreet.

Q: What, then?

A: Oh, heavens, Chief Inspector, you ought to be
able to project yourself into his position.

Q: This is not a position in which I have ever found
myself. You give me the distinct impression that you
were worried.

A: In that case, I wish I had not allowed this
conversation to take place. I was not worried, not worried at all. All I was doing was counselling prudence –
exaggerated prudence, if you like – and that's something that he normally applied himself without having
to be told by me or anyone else.

Q: But this time his behaviour was exceptional?

A: You must not read that sort of meaning into my
words.

Q: The meaning is there, surely?

A: No, it is not. Things were relaxed because of the
nature of the play. They could not help but be.

Q: And you thought that this relaxed atmosphere
was dangerous for him?

A: No more than might make me say, more as a kind
of a joke than anything else, 'Watch it, Simon!'

Q: And *did* he watch it?

A: Latterly, he was convinced that Davina had been
the one behind the sabotage of the play – and behind
the Colonel's death. That put him in a different
relationship with her altogether.

Q: Self-appointed private investigator?

A: Not at all. He was just trying to make up his mind
whether it was worth bothering you people or not.

Gleed had left him alone to read and told him to call him
when he was ready to make his comments. Kenworthy
put this off and put it off again, read through the file a
second and a third time, and certain of the statements
several times more.

Then, alone in that standard issue interview room,
Kenworthy thumped the table. And as he thumped,
Gleed came in, Gleed with one hand in his pocket, Gleed
with his hair short yet unruly about the crown of his
head.

'Well, Superintendent?'

'This is monstrous. When did you question my wife?'

'I did not *question* her. We had an informal conversation whose gist I noted down immediately afterwards, because it was clear it was too precious to risk forgetting. You're not going to tell me I was outside my rights – or that you'd have done otherwise yourself? And I have made you free of my notes.'

Kenworthy's anger did not immediately subside, but he suppressed the incipient eruption.

'It all makes sense,' Gleed said.

'It makes sense only the way I tell it.'

'Granted. And all this is perfectly compatible with your statements. You have omitted nothing of this.'

'But these witnesses take everything out of context. And you yourself have removed most of what context was left.'

'I told you, it is a file *for* you, not *on* you.'

'The original statements must be available to anyone working on the case.'

Kenworthy paused for a difficult moment.

'Has Clingo seen any of this?'

'Clingo? What do you take me for? Clingo's gone, thank God. Clingo's walk-on part in this case is over. If you ask me, Clingo's demands upon Clingo will never overwork the man.'

'He told me he has Kevin O'Shea. A couple of days ago in Nuneaton.'

'That's right. Clingo's angle was that he had heard O'Shea's name and description, in a different place and different company, in connection with an illegal immigrant transit line. There was very little in it. O'Shea is a self-portrait of the Wild Irish Rover: feckless, glib, and a small-scale opportunist. Somewhere back along the line he came across a family of illicit Pakis on the move and for a small consideration found them temporary accommodation in a cantonment he knew of. There's no evidence that he made a habit of it – or that there was any opportunity to repeat the performance at Spentlow

Grange. He was only a transient member of this company. Kevin O'Shea doesn't advance our case at all.
Should we need him, he's remanded in custody. And of
course, he is one up to Clingo. Clingo was very pleased
with himself.'

Gleed flicked through the file.

'I don't understand what you're trying to get at, as far
as I'm concerned,' Kenworthy said.

'Just letting you know the score.'

'This isn't a score. These are just punters' notions.'

'And it all rings so true that I don't disbelieve a word
of it. Of the total version, I mean – your version.'

'I must say you've arrived there by roundabout
means.'

'I've shown you all this so you'll know why I can't give
you a watching brief, not even unofficially. This has been
upstairs. Obviously, it had to. And we have Elder
Statesmen who wouldn't wear it. Having said which,
may I quickly add that I know your work well – have
always taken good care to.'

He paused, and let his eyes drill into Kenworthy's.
Both men had irises of a particularly brilliant blue.

'If I might use you as a sounding-board?' Gleed asked.

'Sound ahead. Bugger the Elder Statesmen. They are
paid to be cautious. Perhaps it's as well that someone is.'

'As I see it, Kenworthy, the night Davina Stott was
locked out, she went to one of three places. And I accept
without hesitation your theory that she let you get out of
earshot because, for fair reason or foul – perhaps just out
of her perpetual self-dramatization – she did not want
you to cotton on to her destination. She went either to
Dunderdale, or to Jesse Allsop, or to the Beaker Folk.'

Kenworthy gave no sign that he had any reservations.
He simply sat and listened.

'Let me develop those possibilities one at a time. On
several levels of probability, I'd be ready to plump for
Dunderdale. She was *persona grata* at the vicarage at all

reasonable hours, and, in case of emergency, could have got away with unreasonable ones. We have Dunderdale's own statement that he was up late. He was accustomed to hearing her complex confessions, both real and affected. But Dunderdale was by now coming round to the belief that Davina Stott was the one who was trying to capsize his Gabbitas Week. Though he'd not yet heard from the other youngsters how she had returned without her dog, the evening the Colonel slipped. We, by the way, have impeccable statements on that point. Also, in the Stott girl's belongings, amid the fluff at the bottom of her school satchel, we have found a three-inch hacksaw blade from whose teeth Forensic have identified filings from the spotlight bracket. And behind the Stotts' bungalow we have found a small trowel about which all we can say is that it has been recently used, abraded against stone and wiped clean. But don't let me leap about. Dunderdale, that Friday night, had no such evidence. He only suspected. Gabbitas Week meant everything to him. Suppose she did call on him late. Suppose he accused her. After all, less than an hour previously, you yourself had done the same thing. Perhaps she said something circumstantial that hit him on the raw. Perhaps she started slinging her sex at him. The last straw had to come sooner or later.'

He looked at Kenworthy for encouragement; and got the poker face.

'So Dunderdale loses his temper, goes for her. He's big enough and strong enough to choke her single-handed. He's powerful enough to have carried her under his cloak all the way to Dogtooth. He lays her on the Anathema doorstep – to befog the whole issue. And the choice of spot is in keeping with his obsessions.'

'Don't forget,' Kenworthy said, 'that the pathologist thought that two people carried the body.'

'The pathologist thought that two people *might* have. But let's move on to Jesse Allsop. A strange man. An unbalanced mixture. A vicious spiral of vicious spirals. And the deeper he's retreated within himself, the harder it's been for him to escape. I've talked to Jesse Allsop a lot – and listened to him. Whether he had any part or not in Davina Stott's death, it's an event that has purged him. Picture the sort of friendship he had with her: the pound-pinching recluse with his hankerings after other things; the precocious schoolgirl befriending him, to meet a dare and to see, within her own pathological twists, how far she can push him. Jesse Allsop's not articulate about it. We can't expect him to be. My own guess is that she threw so much sex at him that he stopped her visits to protect himself. But if that's how they broke up, is it conceivable that she would suddenly call at his house again, 'knock him up in the night?'

'Entirely conceivable. She had some very convenient characteristics. One of them was the ability to forget anything that interfered with the purpose of the moment.'

'And you think she might have provoked him intolerably?'

'If she did, we shall never know more about it than Jesse might tell us.'

'So let me come finally to the Beaker Folk. I was up half the night with three of them, and have ended up with a single charge that would hardly be worth a notch under Clingo's barrel.'

'So our char has told us.'

'So soon? I found John Horrocks a strangely reasonable and fairminded man, though he has – or perhaps it would be truer to say that he had – a quite pathetic faith in that squalid social experiment.'

'I'll agree with the past tense. He must know now that it could never have worked with the rag, tag and bobtail that they have in tow. For my money, it's the girl-friend who's blindly committed; and Horrocks is blindly committed through her.'

'My impression, too; but more to the point – might Davina have gone there that night – it was cold, possibly going to rain again – with the prospect of at least a roof and a sympathetic hearing from Horrocks? As well as teacher, he appears to have been mentor and protector.'

'It depends,' Kenworthy said. 'It depends on what happened that other night – the night she nearly bit off more than she could chew with Kevin O'Shea.'

Gleed looked at him with a sudden irrepressible touch of self-satisfaction.

'You know the details?' Kenworthy asked hopefully.

'Nothing certain. Nothing even workably reliable – because this was a schism buried deep in the politics of the Beaker Folk. Even Horrocks hasn't penetrated the facts to his satisfaction. But I must say he was convincingly candid with me last night. And he told me he'd called you in as catalyst, to try to get the truth to gel.'

'You arrived half an hour too soon.'

'Sorry about that. But we can't put the clock back. Anyway, what Horrocks thinks happened is that Davina, ripe but inexperienced, was pushing things fine with O'Shea – '

'Brinkwomanship.'

'With a poor sense of timing. She was nearly raped by O'Shea, saved at the post by an incursion of women; O'Shea's harem, Horrocks called them. And they set out to teach her the lesson of her life. It was summer-time, and it all took place somewhere in the overgrown grounds of the Grange. The whisper is – and although a lot of it's a tight secret, it's already a kind of folklore in the group – that they stripped the girl of her tee-shirt and jeans – and wiped her gently with nettles: over her ribs and her breasts, her buttocks and thighs – and anywhere else that seemed appropriate. Excruciating pain – and complete humiliation; that's probably why she never breathed a word of complaint. Nobody knows for sure which of the women were concerned. Even Horrocks doesn't. But after they'd dealt with Davina, the story goes that they went for O'Shea. But by then O'Shea had gone – the first stage to Nuneaton. The Irish imagination had some idea of what was coming.'

Gleed leaned back and tried to will a reaction out of Kenworthy.

'Any comment?'

'Only what I've said to a long succession of sergeants: that imagination is the most precious and yet the most dangerous of our tools. A theory can be so good that it looks too attractive.'

Gleed waited for him to expand on this; but Kenworthy waited to be asked.

'What I mean is, you've mentioned three places to which she might have gone that night. All highly probable. But don't let that blind you to the possibility that she might have been headed for somewhere quite different.'

'Such as?'

'I don't know: another valuable weapon. You've got to have a don't know clause in this sort of scenario. And you've got to keep reminding yourself that it's there.'

'I agree that that's sound.' But Gleed sounded disappointed.

'Then you've got to bear in mind that whatever her chosen destination, she may never have reached it.'

'What do you know, Kenworthy?'

'I don't know anything. And that's another keen blade in the armoury, remembering how much you don't know. I don't even know for certain that it was O'Shea that Davina was titillating.'

'Who else, then?'

'Why not Horrocks? Surely he's done enough for her to have earned the crush of the century?'

'I can't picture him allowing her to get very far.'

'And I don't think he would. But she might have tried. And if she did, she'd have stirred up a right old nettlebed, wouldn't she?'

'The inscrutable Christine?'

'She'd be worth a few more imaginative minutes,' Kenworthy suggested.

It was late afternoon by the time that Kenworthy was back in Spentlow. Elspeth was out. The boiler was choked solid with stone-cold clinker. The electric light bulb had blown, and he had to go over to the grocery for a replacement. He was served civilly; but only just; or, rather, a trifle too markedly so. A knot of housewives insisted that he jump their queue; they were in there mainly for the gossip – but it was gossip that had dried up immediately he went in. There was no encouragement for him to indulge in small talk, even if he had been in the mood for it, and he was aware of a shrewd hostility in every pair of eyes that rested on his. It would break out into words the moment he set foot again across the Green; but he would never know (unless Mrs Scadbolt were to tell him) what those words might be. He bought a two-hundred-watt bulb. That would throw up a fresh drabness in the once-yellow wallpaper.

It was after five when Elspeth returned. He had forgotten that it was the afternoon of her talk to the Women's Institute. She looked tired, and had unusually little to say for herself. Slowly, and with informative resignation, she tore up the notes of her talk and dropped them, a pinch at a time, into a wastepaper bin decorated with reproductions from the walls of Lascaux.

'There are aspects of a detective's wife's life that had not occurred to me after all.' She had been looking forward to giving that talk.

That was all she ever said to him about her failure to make any rapport with the Spentlow women. The honeymoon stage of the Kenworthys' relationship to Spentlow was over.

*

The next day, Kenworthy made another of his early morning excursions, swinging a walking-stick, whistling ebulliently, throwing hearty 'good morning's' over garden gates and walls, whether people cared to know him or not, leaving the village briskly behind him, the very image of a man bound for a long day in the hills.

He went only to Spentlow Grange, past the field in which Jesse Allsop's tractor and trailer still lay over-turned. But he did not go up as far as the commune's main drive and lodge gates. He crept into the grounds along a narrow track that, to judge from the specialized debris that lay scattered about one of its rare grassier patches, was a favourite courting-walk of Spentlow's summer visitors. He came after a quarter of a mile into thickening woodland, and was soon lost amongst trees, and safely out of sight of the great house.

He came soon to an intersection of tracks, there being another well-pounded footpath which led down a shallow valley as an alternative and circuitous route back into Spentlow, swinging round a copse-scattered slope to a distant spidering limb of the village.

Kenworthy moved slowly now, taking as much care of his footfalls as a tracking Indian. After several abortive inspections of the land on either side of him he began to move circumspectly towards the house, coming at last into a clearing amongst the trees bounded on one side by a neglected yew hedge that marked the boundary of one of the great lawns. It was here that a quarter of a century's rubbish had been tipped: not merely, nor even mainly, that of the Beaker Folk, who seldom walked even as far as this from their quarters to dispose of their garbage. But there was stuff left by casual campers – as well as evidence of earlier squatters: mattresses, bicycle frames stripped of anything with the most optimistic of mechanical futures, beer-cans, wheel-less prams, pram-less wheels. Corned beef, condensed milk, cardboard packets ravaged by storms. On two sides of the glade there were banks of old nettles, the year's crop, blackened by frosts, straggling and overgrown. And it was here, caught casually amongst the dead bottom stalks, that he found what he was looking for: the last three pages of Davina's *Anathema Stone* script.

CHAPTER XIV

The same afternoon, he went down to see Jesse Allsop again. The day was indolent and ashen, and he announced to Elspeth that he thought he would go down and offer their landlord a little advice about his letting practices. The village was deserted as he walked through it, and if there was anyone lurking to speculate on his motives their secret was well kept. The farmyard was exactly as it had been left after the scrabbling out of the Stone; an asymmetrical gash under the front door, a hoist of sorts assembled on a tripod of old piping.

Allsop was busy at an afternoon's officework in his parlour. Box-files of correspondence from putative customers were spilling out over an antique table top. A table of next year's weeks, plotted against the fanciful names of his caravans, was pinned to a square of hardboard: Casa Nostra, Elfin View, Sunset Corner. There was a stack of duplicated specifications of his cottages beside a pile of cheap manilla envelopes. But there was nothing of caprice or vitality in the spirit in which he was tackling his work. He was plodding through it in the same slow lumbering fashion in which one of his neighbours might have addressed a root crop with his hoe. There was about him none of the fire and fright that had moved him to try to shift the curse from his premises. He did not look like a man who had recently undergone a harrowing experience; he looked like a man whose crisis, now past, seemed barely credible. His window looked across the catastrophic yard, and, from where he was sitting, his eyes, whenever he raised them, must have caught sight of the wreckage where the Stone had been. If he had wanted to avoid the reminder, there were a number of places to which he could easily have moved his chair. But Jesse Allsop, sombre as ever, dark-shadowed about cheeks and chin, glossily groomed about his head, seemed to have extricated himself unscathed from events. It was as if certain things had never happened, Davina Stott amongst them.

If Kenworthy had wanted to make a few gentlemanly suggestions to Jesse Allsop about his shortcomings as a landlord, the way was signposted for him by the litter on the table. But Kenworthy did not talk about open-air holidays.

'There are one or two things I want to tidy up, Jesse, if you'll forgive my intrusion on your time. I'd like to see the layout of your bedroom, and the window from which you first saw the girl's body.'

Allsop nodded vacantly, not pleased by the request, but evidently not minded to argument or obstruction. Nor did it appear to strike him that the demand was at odds with Kenworthy's frequent assertion that he had no concern in the case. He led the way up a respectably carpeted staircase, past gloomy oil-paintings of the dales in the days of Walton and Cotton, to a landing whose window commanded a flanking view of the yard and the site of the Stone. Allsop jerked his head as if he were making him a present of the view; an angle of the yard very similar to that they would have used in the play. From here Allsop could indeed have had a perfect view of the corpse.

There were sounds of other activity on this upstairs floor, and through an open bedroom door Kenworthy caught sight of a middle-aged woman ironing. She looked up as they passed, startled for a moment, as if the very act of plying an iron were an illicit activity. Jesse

Allsop paid no attention to her, but led Kenworthy straight to his own bedroom, which was vast, fusty and innocent of conscious design. Kenworthy did no more than put his head round the door, made an exaggerated business of not being interested in the intricacies of the room, looked only briefly in the direction of the window. Then he asked if he might go to the lavatory, to which Allsop took him: a hair-cracked porcelain pedestal, with rust stains running down from the screws in the heavy wooden seat. When he came out again, Allsop was talking to the woman, but had not gone into the room with her, and she had not come away from her ironing board. Kenworthy recognized her by sight, but did not know her name. She had been doing some odd jobs in the Hall at their rehearsals.

'You normally go out of your way to look out of the landing window when you get up in the night?'

Kenworthy nodded suggestively at the geographical arrangement of the bedroom and lavatory doors. A trip across the landing was an unnecessary excursion.

'Sometimes, if it's a nice night. Or if I'm interested in tomorrow's weather.'

'You can see precisely the same view from your own room.'

'My curtains are always drawn at night. These never are.'

'You didn't walk across the landing because of something you'd heard, or thought you'd heard?'

'No. There was bright moonlight falling in, and I went to look out.'

Kenworthy seemed to accept that. They went back down into the parlour and Allsop asked if he should get his daily woman to make them a pot of tea. Kenworthy declined, and Allsop did not press. But suddenly, as Kenworthy was within half a step of leaving the room, the morose little farmer made a dive into a lower shelf of a glass-fronted bookcase.

'Now, here's something – '

It was an impulse, a decision on which he had been sitting undetermined throughout Kenworthy's visit. And it was something which, all but for a split second, might never have come Kenworthy's way.

'Here's something from the Gabbitas papers that never did get into Dunderdale's hands.'

It was a black-bound inch-thick notebook, its pages interleaved with all kinds of *incunabula* and printed forms of memorial services, invitations, formal notes from parishioners and the like. Allsop opened it out at a particular page, which he had no difficulty in finding.

'This is something that Gertrude took with her when she went into the hills. It was something I could never understand, when I was young, why she should run away from a man, and yet take such a personal slice of him with her. But I know now only too well. None of us knows what we really do want, do we? But you read that. If Dunderdale had known I'd got this, he could have brought out a damned sight better new *Hob* book.'

The handwriting was pinched and ineffectively ornate, the loops entangled in fuzzy flourishes that did nothing for them. Whole paragraphs of scribble had been decisively crossed out. There was a tentative sketch of prototype goblins, their lower limbs incomplete, but no attempt, at this draft stage, to conceal the imperfections.

'That's a story that Wilbur Gabbitas never did finish.'

In point of fact, it was not a story at all, but the sketchiest of foundation notes for one. A stranger had come into the land of Hob's people and taken to wife a woman of the Sopalls. She was beautiful, contrary, talented, constricted, misunderstood not only by her own kindred but even by herself. But under the influence of the stranger she discovered herself, became known far and wide for her grace and great gifts; until, that is, she was driven away; driven away by the women of the land. Gabbitas had left the briefest of notions why, which he had never found it in himself to develop: long silences when she went to the shops; witches' laughter round walls and corners; faithful friends suddenly tainted by the mob.

'Now you know,' Allsop said, 'why Gertrude fled. And you asked me the other day why it was that Davina Stott stopped coming here. I can tell you. It was because of the damned women.'

'Which women?' Kenworthy asked.

'A man shouldn't be asked to name names. When people gang together they aren't single people any longer. They aren't individuals.'

'I think you ought to give me a hint or two, all the same. You want this thing cleared up.'

'*I* don't want it cleared up. It'll never be cleared up. As soon as one part is cleared, another corner will darken. Besides – you don't need to be told.'

Kenworthy nodded.

He walked energetically back to the cottage: fallen leaves were clinging dispiritedly to the damp pavements.

'Well – have you got the wicked landlord to mend his wicked ways?'

Elspeth, too, was ironing.

'No. But I noticed that he has a double bed, made up with two pillows, the linen freshly laundered. And a woman about the place about whom he has nothing to say.'

'I'll make a few enquiries,' Elspeth said. 'Though in Spentlow's present mood, I expect there'll be tight lips. Still, there's always Mrs Scadbolt. She knows everything.'

'It would be interesting to know whether there was a woman on the premises on the night Davina was killed.'

'I dare say that practically everyone in Spentlow will know.'

CHAPTER XV

That same evening he decided that, press-men or no, and whatever the state of his popularity in the village, he was going to have a beer. But, not for the first time since he had come here, his road to the Recruiting Sergeant was delayed by the sight of lights across the Green.

He saw them as he came out of the cottage gate: great, bright shining oblongs that exaggerated the shadows of the church buttresses, the square lines of the primary school and the Tudor chimneys of the vicarage. It was exactly as if the play was in full rehearsal again, and such a notion was supported by the activity in the forecourt of the Hall, in which a great many cars seemed to be parked.

When Kenworthy had made it clear that he did not intend to go on with his part in the play it had given a great jolt to the vicar's committee. At an emergency meeting three members had reversed their previous votes, and Dunderdale had had to resign himself to holding off the play for a year or two, if not for all time.

Kenworthy set off towards the oasis of bustle and light. As he neared the Hall, he saw that one of the parked vehicles was the outside broadcast van of a television company, and that a thick trail of cable was leading in through the main entrance.

He gave the front door a wide berth, and picked his way through the churchyard in order to approach the Hall from the rear. There was a small kitchen behind the stage, and through its window, thanks to a mercifully open door, he was able to see about two-thirds of what was happening on the platform.

The scene had been set for the first encounter between

Gabbitas and Gertrude in the Dogtooth yard – but far
more comprehensively than at any rehearsal in which he
himself had taken part. The backcloth was in position,
and at right angles to it a canvas flat showed part of the
wing of the farmhouse. The bales of straw were in position, as was a realistic representation of the pump.
Christine, as Gertrude, was wearing full make-up,
including a tangled black wig. The intention was precisely the same as Davina's had been in the part, but the
personality presented looked utterly different. Christine
was taller, for one thing, and the short ragged dress she
was wearing brought out the lines of a bosom that normally seemed to have disappeared beneath the rebel-
lious shabbiness that she affected. She had made up her
face to suggest country diet and healthy weathering, and
had somehow contrived to give it a wholly more rounded
look. The effect, in fact, was not only to give a quite
startlingly satisfying evocation of Gertrude, but also a
totally new conception of Christine.

Gabbitas was being played by Horrocks himself, in a
tight-fitting dark clerical suit. He had the exact figure for
the part, which he acted with a sense of identification
that made nonsense of the efforts of previous amateurs.
Kenworthy, in his mid-forties, could only have delivered
his lines as a well-intentioned ham, however well-served
he had been by cosmetician and costumier; and God
knows what a ludicrous figure Colonel Noakes must
have cut.

But this pair had the professional touch. Christine,
especially, had in her acting a precision that made it
clear that she must have done a great deal of secret
preparation. She knew the part inside out, and there was
nothing tentative about her movements and gestures.
One had seen hints of discernible genius in Davina's
handling of the role; but in Christine's performance it
was discipline and training that came out – a self-
control, a sense of purpose, and a devotion of effort of

which it was hard to believe her capable. She was not one of those actresses whose impulsive interpretation of a character might change with the mood of the day. She gave the impression that if she raised her arm from the elbow on a certain syllable, that was the way she would have played the moment throughout the longest of runs.

And she was playing to an audience. Not only the television team, but every reporter still left in the village was in the Hall, some of them leaping from time to time on to the stage with their cameras and a frenzy of flash-light bulbs – to which both actors seemed impervious.

Kenworthy gave up his stealthy pretence, went in through the door of the little kitchen, crept through the shadows of the wings, circled out of range of the battery of stage-lighting, and joined the small miscellaneous crowd who had gathered behind the television cameras. He found himself next to a man he had known slightly as the assistant stage manager.

'Not thinking of going it alone, are they?'

'I don't see how they could. There are too many parts that they never could fill. I think this is just a publicity stunt.'

'Spentlow's going to be glued to its television screens.'

Then the television producer called for silence, and asked for a re-run of the whole scene. It went through without hitch – the passionate kisses of the primitive Gertrude, the diffidence of the overwhelmed curate. The wit of some of the lines came over with a beauty of timing that raised a laugh even from the blasé technicians.

When it was over, the lights were on in the body of the Hall, a man without either camera or note-pad stood up and pushed his way to the stage. He was elderly, with dirtily greying yellow hair, and he climbed on to the stage, extending his hand to Christine in congratulation. There was no doubting her pleasure. It suffused her face in a manner that hardly seemed credible in contrast to her customary sick hatred of everything on which her eye seemed to light.

Kenworthy removed himself from the Hall before he could be approached by any of the principals. In view of the new influx of media-men into the village he decided to give the pub a miss yet again. But when he got home he announced to Elspeth that he felt restless and thought that an extended nocturnal walk would do him good.

'Have I my gloves here?' he asked. 'Or did we leave them in the car?'

She knew exactly where to put her hands on them.

'I made a point of leaving nothing in the car.'

She also noticed that he slipped his bedroom slippers into the pocket of his raincoat.

'It's going to be that sort of walk, is it?'

'Just might want to rest my feet,' he said shamelessly.

'For God's sake watch it, Simon.'

Next morning, Mrs Scadbolt brought the news that Christine had been visited in the Hall last night by a talent scout. He had been very impressed by her performance, and as a result of it, she and Horrocks would be leaving the village when he had worked out his notice at the school. They were going to join a travelling company that went round the country giving shows to children.

'And good riddance too, I reckon,' she said. 'That'll be the end of the Beaker Folk.'

CHAPTER XVI

The Kenworthys' time in Spentlow followed its natural course, and they came to the final stretch, which with a more peaceful prelude would have been Gabbitas Week. Only three items of the original arrangements were allowed to remain, and the first of these was the Mock Auction, which took place in the Hall on their last

Saturday but one in the village. It was carried out with
such vigour and financial success that no one would have
thought that any of the leading figures had anything on
their minds. Dunderdale managed to turn on a tap of
false merriment, and bullied his customers mercilessly.
The sale was carried out along lines that must have
seemed mad to any strangers present: the bidder had to
put his money down, and it was forfeit if he was outbid. It
made nonsense of serious buying, and could only have
been possible on a special occasion, when a community
has come together with the happy intention of giving
money away. But that seemed to be the spirit of
Spentlow today. There was a turn-out from all levels of
society – from the Pack Horse to the Recruiting Sergeant
– even from the Grange. Christine made a bid for an
item, and for £5 acquired the ornate base of a treadle
sewing machine.

The euphoria which had inspired her test performance of the Gertrude scene seemed to have stayed with
her. She could scarcely have been called beautiful – in
any case, the way she dressed went a long way to neut-
ralizing any such pretensions that she might have had.
But she was even wearing garish clothes this afternoon –
quietly purple slacks and a roll-necked sweater. There
was less of her hair over her face than usual, and her
more relaxed mood even permitted her the ghost of a
smile at Kenworthy.

They watched davenports, tallboys, what-nots and
umbrella stands transferred into the hands of generous
bidders. The compulsion to be charitable in public
seemed to have unlocked the purse-strings. The last
thing to go was a rather beautiful Edwardian workbox,
and Elspeth secured it for two pounds.

'There is one other piece of business still to transact.'

The two churchwardens were stacking and checking
the money that had been put down on one of the Boys'

Brigade drums. Dunderdale led the way out across the Green into the main street, where he waited for a semi-circle to form round him outside Barton Brightmore's window, on which he rapped imperatively with his knuckles.

'One mahogany cloak-tree, disputed property of the Allsop and Brightmore families. Donated by Jesse Allsop. And I am sure that our friend Barton Brightmore will want to assert the family honour by confirming that the object is given to the cause.'

Barton Brightmore had by now come to his door: an inarticulate and ratty little man, a cabinet-maker by persuasion, who did not even get as far as opening his mouth.

'An elegant amenity for any household, ladies and gentlemen. What am I bid for this beautifully hand-turned eighteenth-century piece?'

There was a chill wind blowing across the Green. Coat collars were turned up, labouring men's hands with-drawn into their cuffs. People were slow with their opening offers. Maybe this was something that Spentlow preferred to leave to the spokesmen of the main antagonists.

'A pound.'

This was from a resident of The Close, the small and never finished estate on Allsop land that had not been one of the developer's successes. There were only one or two people from The Close at the sale, and their presence seemed to have done no more than persuade the real Spentlow to keep its treasures to itself.

'Put your money down, then, please, sir.'

Someone manoeuvred in the drum, which had somehow been left on the perimeter of the crowd.

'Ten pounds.' Heads were turned, and it was seen that Jesse Allsop – who had not been present at the main part of the sale – had come quietly up from his farm.

'Fifteen.'

Barton Brightmore had slipped indoors and come out with his wallet.

'Seventeen fifty.'

It was Dunderdale himself who had now entered the bidding. 'Twenty.'

'Twenty-five.'

'Twenty-seven fifty.'

'Thirty.'

Barton Brightmore had to write an I.O.U. He was light of seventy pounds already, whether he retained the stand or not. The bidding went on until he had offered fifty, and then Jesse Allsop's caution seemed to get the better of his sentiment; the vicar had dropped out at thirty-five.

'Fifty-two and a half.'

This was a new voice, feminine and metallic; one familiar to the Kenworthys.

'Mrs Scadbolt.'

'I think the best thing I can do,' she said, 'is put my Post Office book on the drum.'

She seemed to be a lone figure in the crowd, no hat on the incongruously piled black hair, the ill-conceived rouge on her cheeks at odds with the dismal afternoon. Most of the other spectators were in families or couples, but although Mrs Scadbolt's shoulders were pressed up against those of her neighbours, one could see that she was alone.

'Mrs Scadbolt, fifty-two pounds fifty, pledged with a Post Office book. I might say, ladies and gentlemen, that the going rate for such a lovely piece in the West End sale-rooms these days would be at least a hundred and twenty.'

But Spentlow was not the West End. It was an incredible madness that had got into the village that afternoon. At one moment it had looked as if the Allsops and Brightmores would have gone on lavishing their savings astronomically for the sake of their pride; for possession of something that surely neither side could desperately want for its own sake. Then, equally suddenly, their economic hard-headedness had prevailed. They had thrown enough away. They might be able to persuade themselves that it was in a good cause to which they would have contributed in any case. But Jesse Allsop and Barton Brightmore had shown no doubt about where they were going to draw their line. The crowd relapsed into a tense silence when Mrs Scadbolt entered the lists.

An auction conducted along such lines was not a serious commercial occasion; it was a family excuse for reckless charity in front of one's friends and enemies. To enter the bidding late for the sake of sheer gain was not playing the game. There was tension in the silence that followed Mrs Scadbolt's bid; yet no one seemed minded to better it. Dunderdale looked at the two main contestants: Jesse Allsop was looking vacantly into space; Barton Brightmore's eyes were fixed on the back of another man's neck.

'Going to Mrs Scadbolt – '

Mrs Scadbolt was standing granite-faced and apparently friendless. It was difficult to tell how committed she was to winning the hat-stand. And, of course, it was impossible to know how she would stand up to the financial loss if she failed; women like her sometimes had surprising little nest-eggs.

Dunderdale looked hopefully at the now silent faces, but Spentlow was no longer interested.

Then Kenworthy spoke.

'Fifty-five.'

Mrs Scadbolt looked uncertainly round the crowd, as if seeking moral support. But no eyes were prepared to meet hers.

Dunderdale beamed on Kenworthy, as if he were doing the community a service by keeping the thing out of Mrs Scadbolt's hands. Kenworthy got out his chequebook. Mrs Scadbolt moistened her lips with the tip of her tongue. Her eyes moved, barely perceptibly. Without moving her head, she looked first at one face in the crowd, then at another. Then she shrugged her shoulders, as if involuntarily, turned on her heel and pushed her way through the crowd and out of it.

'Going to Mr Kenworthy – '

As the crowd thinned out, Kenworthy remained behind to arrange for someone to carry the cloak-tree over to the cottage. He brushed shoulders with Christine, who was making similar arrangements for her sewing machine.

'Congratulations!'

She beamed on him; not a timorous smile this time.

'I hope that this is the beginning of a new and altogether happier spell of life for you,' he said.

'I'm sure it will be.' Complete freedom from tension, as if she had thrown something off.

'Pity, though, I never had the chance to play Wilbur to your Gertrude.'

'Please don't let me give you the impression that I think you owe me an explanation – '

Elspeth was in fact not being acid; good humoured, mock ironic – and trustful; but curious to get at the facts.

'I have a distinct memory that we decided we could not afford a hire-car for the rest of the holiday. Oh, I know that fifty-five pounds won't actually break the bank – '

'Especially if we can part with it at the going rate. That would make sixty-five profit – '

'I doubt very much, Simon, whether that was uppermost in your mind. As a matter of fact, I rather like the piece. I'd like us to keep it, if we can see our way to it.'

'I had thought to trying a claim on expenses for it. I know that's a bit awkward, since I'm not specifically on the case – in fact, I'm specifically off it. All the same, I dare say that Gleed – '

'Expenses?'

But Kenworthy was reluctant to explain himself until they were behind the privacy of their front door.

'It dawned on me suddenly that Mrs Scadbolt was only bidding as leader of a ring. And I suddenly knew that the most important thing of this whole afternoon was to know who was in that ring. Did you follow her eyes as she hesitated whether to go another sixty? I didn't think they would, because once they knew I was in the running they would not expect me to drop out.'

He waited.

'Who?' Elspeth asked at last.

'An interesting little circle. The vicar's housekeeper for one.'

'Mrs Doreen Malkin.'

'The creature with the earrings like dustbin lids.'

'Geraldine Cartwright.'

'Then there was the woman who used to do for Colonel Noakes.'

'Alice Brightmore.'

'And last of all the woman who appears to share Jesse Allsop's bed now and then.'

'Emmeline Malkin.'

'Four of them. The Scadbolt unobtrusively caught their eyes one after another. And each of them signalled No. An interesting little bunch. At least, they interest me. With one exception, they were all signatories of those nasty little statements that Gleed had in my own special file.'

'You don't surprise me. Shall I surprise you?'

Elspeth was very near to a broad smile.

'You can try.'

'They are also the vigilantes. Don't you remember, I told you when we first came here, that there was a little group so scandalized by the Beaker Folk that they appointed themselves to keep an eye on things? Like peeping through uncurtained windows at the Grange. All except Geraldine Cartwright, that is. She is a great fashioner of ammunition for others to fire. But I can't see her joining in any field-work on wet nights.'

'Thank you,' Kenworthy said. 'All highly suggestive. It's time I got Gleed on the phone.'

'He'll be glad to know you're awake.'

CHAPTER XVII

'The eighteenth century, ladies and gentlemen; the age of enlightenment.'

And then, without comment, Dunderdale showed on the screen a series of transparencies, blown up from old prints and sketch-books. Spentlow was delighted. Sprawling middens, tottering earth-closets, disintegrating hovels – and a fading water-colour primitive, probably authentic, of the yard at Dogtooth before Thomas Allsop acquired the Stone.

The village had shown up in force for the vicar's lecture. It was hard to think that anyone was missing, except the halt and the sick. *Bygone Spentlow* was close to the listeners' hearts, and *The Second Book of Hob*, on sale at the door, was in great demand. Dunderdale concentrated for ten minutes on poverty, squalor and the determination to survive. But it was not long before the first Allsops and Brightmores were on the scene. Thomas Allsop, he who had seized the Stone, had knitted eyebrows and an embroidered waistcoat. His contemporary, old Thaddaeus Brightmore, was dressed in soiled rags that appeared to be held together by knots, string and abiding trust in miracle.

'Believe it or not, ladies and gentlemen, this Allsop and that Brightmore were friends.'

A restrained titter. The lights were out, so Kenworthy

could not see which of the committed infighters were the first to allow themselves to relax. Jesse Allsop had come in, and little Barton Brightmore was sitting with his family a couple of rows away. The vicar's target was clearly a lasting armistice.

'Friends, that is, until they began to compete in the scientific spirit of the age. To put a name to their speciality, they were Resurrectionists.'

He screened a shot of the smooth-worn bier that still stood within the bell-tower of St Giles.

'And I hope there is no one here who thinks that a Resurrectionist was some kind of fiery evangelical. Thomas Allsop and Thaddaeus Brightmore were practical men. The corpses that they raised, for a sovereign a time, were destined for medical research. Anatomy was in vogue as an experimental science, and the workhouses and public morgues could not stay abreast of the demands of doctors. Allsop and Brightmore applied themselves with fervour.'

Much of this must have been known in detail to the audience, but Dunderdale's tone implied that he had more details in reserve.

'Thomas and Thaddaeus were terrible and efficient partners – Arthur James Rankin, Matilda Foulds, Jeremiah Malkin and Ebenezer Scadbolt were amongst those whose bodies disappeared from this churchyard of ours before the grave had had time to corrupt. In the case of Caleb Mycock, the mourners cast their dust and ashes on a coffin ballasted with stones before the cortège departed from the dead man's cottage.'

Dunderdale brought on an artist's impression of Hob's Kitchen before the stones of the barrow had fallen.

'So far we have been talking of the Allsops and the Brightmores at a time when there was nothing in their souls but sweetness and light. Alas, they were soon to enter into rivalry. The two principal clients for Allsop-Brightmore produce were a Dr William Baines of Shef-

field and a Dr T. Armstrong Bramwell of Derby. And
Thomas Allsop, having heard theories that the three-
cornered mound was an ancient burial chamber, saw
hopes of a new source of merchandise. The removal of
one of the cornerstones to his yard was a mere incidental.
What Thomas Allsop had not realized is that the human
skeleton, deprived by time and decay of its ligaments,
does not hold together with that obliging integrity post-
ulated by the grotesque illustrators of irresponsible fic-
tions. All that he could do was to fill a linen bag with as
many bones as he could gather. And that is how the
remain of an eminent man, a Bronze Age Chieftain,
came t change hands at the back door of a Derby
surgery at the knock-down price of half a crown.'
    The picture changed to a photograph of the mahogany
cloak-tree.
    'And so, you see, we move nearer home. Dr Bramwell,
refusing more than a nominal fee for Thomas Allsop's
bag of bones, nevertheless prevailed upon him hence-
forth to operate independently, with a promise of bon-
uses if he could ensure that no more bodies were wasted
on the obscurantist medical schools of Sheffield. From
now on, the Allsops and the Brightmores worked in
bitter opposition. And if there had already been macabre
scenes by night in Spentlow's acre of rest, the traffic now
became complex indeed. There was trickery afoot, even
running fights in the byways after disinterment. It
became the acme of business acumen to take possession
of a corpse after you had let a rival family do the digging.'
    The vicar tapped the image of the hat-stand with his
pointer.
    'The professional rivalry between the Brightmores
and the Allsops went on for some fifteen years. At times
when the death rate in Spentlow was too low to ensure
economic viability, excursions would be made to other
settlements – to Hartington and Tissington, and even as
far afield as Alstonefield and Longnor. But at last Thad-

daeus Brightmore, the older and less firm of the two, had a premonition of his own approaching end, and began to be haunted by the thought that his own mortal shell might find its way on an Allsop wagon to the dissecting table. He accordingly summoned courage, dismissed pride and went on a diplomatic mission to Dogtooth. His proposition was that Thomas Allsop should have twenty golden sovereigns here and now, and another twenty one month after the event, together with three articles of his own choice from amongst the Brightmore heirlooms, in return for an assurance that his, Thaddaeus's remains should be held sacred. A deed was signed. Thomas Allsop collected his cloak-tree and two other pieces which we can no longer account for. Yet at dawn on the morrow of Thaddaeus's burial, his mound was found torn open.'

Dunderdale paused for effect. Somewhere in the Hall a baby in arms began to cry.

'Ladies and gentlemen, I do not believe that Thomas Allsop would ever have been guilty of the gross deception which his contemporaries and posterity have ascribed to him. Would he have let himself in for a night's hard labour and the certain loss of his second instalment of twenty pounds? Was not Thaddaeus Brightmore more probably the victim of a Malkin or a Scadbolt – or, as seems to me most likely – of some vengeful soul from as far afield as Hartington, Tissington, Alstonefield or Longnor?'

Kenworthy crept out whilst knots of people were still gossiping in the precincts of the Hall. In the Recruiting Sergeant as he had expected, he found old Billy Brightmore, the landlord, holding the fort of the yellow-plastered bar.

'Well, Superintendent – do we know the truth now?'
'We have laughed our sides sore over it.'
'And is it going to make a sliver of difference?'

'It ought.'

'It ought for sure. The sort of fighting we've had here for as long as I can remember is bad for a place. Full marks to Dunderdale if he's put an end to it.'

He did not add, did not perhaps fully grasp, that he had all his life been as active as any in the internecine warfare.

It was only a few minutes later that the usual clientele began to arrive for their usual pints. They were all either Brightmores or neutrals, but all full of the lecture, and repeating bits of it to each other with relish. Dunderdale came in with Horrocks and Christine. They joined Kenworthy, who had placed himself safely out of eavesdropping range of the main gathering. Dunderdale was physically and mentally elated by the success of his talk; at the same time inclined to philosophize, and clearly already beginning to feel the reaction of emptiness that follows the completion of a big task.

'So this time next week, you'll be gone, Mr Kenworthy. And you two others, I expect, will be moving into lodgings nearer John's work, until he finishes his term.'

Horrocks nodded.

'So you leave the world to darkness and to me? Spentlow is going to be a singularly empty place.'

'Surely Spentlow's greatest claim to fame is still to happen?' Horrocks asked. 'I'm very conscious of the lull before the storm. Everything that matters is hanging fire. Even the press has grown tired. I don't know why the place isn't still crawling with policemen.'

'My feeling too,' Dunderdale said. 'I don't understand the inaction.'

They were all looking at Kenworthy as if they held him responsible for what was not happening.

'And I still think that the play should have gone on,' Dunderdale said. 'Spentlow has lost the chance to stage its first dramatic production since the pageant they had for the Jubilee of 1935. Two full houses: one hundred and twenty seats each. For most of this village, it would have been their first taste of the living theatre, pantomimes excepted. We should have gone through with it. It's like the tradition of persuading the bereaved to touch a cold corpse. It dispels fears and delusions. Why, oh why, did Davina Stott have to wreck it all for us? Sometimes I think I understand, and sometimes I don't.'

'She had to wreck anything that was bigger than herself,' Kenworthy said. 'I have no doubt at all that she was the one who was responsible for the blown fuses, the falling lamps, the stolen scripts : and the attacks on the Colonel.'

'She can surely never have meant to kill him?'

'Of course not. Any more than she meant to injure her father when she tampered with the stair-rods. Ultimate consequences were remote from immediate purpose. But I think she had another reason too – as far as the Colonel was concerned. She could have destroyed the play; she might also have been the making of it.'

'Sorry, Kenworthy – I don't see what you mean.'

'She laid traps for the Colonel because she desperately wanted him out of the cast – and someone else in – '

'But is that reasonable?' Horrocks asked. 'When she conceived those traps, I don't think you'd come on the scene, had you?'

'It wasn't me she wanted as Gabbitas.'

'Who, then?'

'I saw you make a very good job of the part for the sake of Christine's demonstration.'

Horrocks was keen to establish a disclaimer. Dunderdale used a second round of drinks to smooth over embarrassment. And Christine was quick to add that John would never have agreed to play a main part and produce at the same time. Then Kenworthy suddenly changed the subject.

'We still haven't answered the main question of who beat Davina with nettles. You can't tell me you don't have suspicions.'

'Suspicions!' Christine said. 'That was the horrible thing about it. We suspected everyone. It was all so unfair. It ended up with everyone in the commune under a cloud.'

'But if you did not know who did it, how did you even know it had been done?'

'It was all anyone talked about, next morning at breakfast-time. People just seemed to know.'

'I suppose that's how folk legends get off the ground,' Horrocks said. 'Even those about Hob and the Anathema Stone.'

'You see, Mr Kenworthy, some of the women went mad about Kevin O'Shea. He was a bit of a legend himself. It was a joke at first, when Davina looked as if she was after him too. Then it suddenly looked as if she was going to get him. Please don't think I hold any brief for their outlook – '

A day or two ago, it would have been impossible to believe that Christine could talk so reasonably. The success of her stage test seemed to have altered her entire personality.

'I don't think that for a moment. But I do think you must have some idea about who was the ring-leader.'

'I do. I always did have. And I could be totally wrong. That's what makes it so dangerous.'

'You're going to tell us sooner or later,' Kenworthy said. 'It might as well be now.'

'No!'

'I know you all believed in communal property, but there must have been someone who thought of O'Shea as her own.'

'That wouldn't prove anything.'

'Much as I admire your sense of fairness, Christine – '

She smiled at him remotely.

'I hope I am proof against that sort of flattery, Mr Kenworthy.'

Then John Horrocks spoke up.

'You might as well tell him, Christine. You know you are right. And if it serves to clear up the larger issue – '

But she shook her head. So Horrocks simply answered for her.

'You remember the girl Triss, Mr Kenworthy?'

'The difficult one? The one who didn't want to stay in the room, the night I came? The one Christine pushed back into her seat?'

'Triss had fallen for O'Shea in a big way. And she was the one who was fullest of rumours next morning.'

'But could Triss have attacked Davina on her own?' Kenworthy asked.

Christine shrugged her shoulders. She did not seem to resent the way in which Horrocks had pre-empted her. It might even have been a relief to her.

'That lot were a weak-kneed mob. If Triss led the way, she'd have no shortage of helpers.'

'And where is Triss now?'

'Gone away.'

'Gone where?'

'She didn't say. We didn't ask. Perhaps back where she came from, wherever that is.'

'Gone, in fact, wherever good Ultimate Anarchists do go?'

Christine smiled waterily. Then there was a rustle of attention throughout the pub. The door had opened and Jesse Allsop had come in.

He stood for a moment just within the bar, surveying the premises as if he had never entered them in his life before; which, it was later established, was actually the case. Conversation dried up on all sides – including among Kenworthy and his party. Allsop nodded to one or two men, with whom for a lifetime he had not been on speaking terms, but who were characters of such sub-

stance as to be recognized as leaders amongst his
enemies. He went up to the bar. Billy Brightmore served
him a double whisky, and was seen to wave away the
offer of money. Within a few seconds, conversation
struck up again, but in suppressed tones. Billy
Brightmore leaned on his bar and looked benignly out-
wards.

'Your hat-stand fetched a good price, then, Jesse?'

'Success for you, Vicar,' Kenworthy said. 'The object
of the exercise, I take it?'

'It's up to Jesse from now on. I know which way he
wants it.'

'He gave me a tip this afternoon that I thought had
broken the case for me. What Christine just told us has
come as a surprise to me.'

'What was that?'

'A Gabbitas note book that has come down the family
through Gertrude. There was the sketch of a *Hob* story,
suggesting that it was village women who had driven
Gertrude away.'

'So you thought – ?'

Dunderdale was now looking at Kenworthy keenly.

'You're not suggesting – ?'

'That it was village women who were harassing
Davina? I certainly thought it was village women who
had beaten her with nettles.'

Dunderdale was now leaning across the table, keeping
his voice dramatically down.

'I can't think of any woman in this village – '

Kenworthy too spoke quietly, almost the delivery of a
ventriloquist, his eye fixed on Jesse Allsop and the men
who were now talking to him.

'Tell me, Vicar: which woman in this village had most
to lose – or thought she had – when Jesse Allsop started
receiving visits from Davina?'

But Dunderdale was unimpressed.

'Oh, I've known for years, we've all known for years,

that Jesse has a mistress. He's always been discreet, but
never discreet enough to fool Spentlow. Tuesdays and
Saturdays were always her nights. Still are, as far as I
know.'

'And who might have begun to fear for the reputation
of Colonel Noakes?'

'Oh, there I must protest. There was nothing between
the Colonel and Alice Brightmore. She is the gentlest of
creatures, the most law-abiding, the most timorous – '

'Timorous women can change, if they see a certain
kind of threat. And tell me: who is the one woman in
Spentlow sufficiently literate to capture other women's
fancy with the turn of a phrase – a woman to whom
scandal of any kind is so odious that she would not miss
the shadow of it? Although, of course, she would leave
material activity strictly to others – ?'

'There are women like that in any community.'

'And who is the one woman who always says and does
what she thinks fit, irrespective of consequences? Who
was the only one who saw a chance of a mercenary deal
at your Charity Auction – provided she could find
enough shareholders to pool their capital? You followed
her eyes that day, just as I did.'

'Vera Scadbolt is a menace. It did my heart good to
see you frustrate her.'

'Finally – and I make no apologies for asking you this,
Vicar – even for asking you in front of our friends here.
Who was the woman who was most infuriated when
Davina Stott put you yourself into a compromising posi-
tion?'

Dunderdale actually blushed. And then lost his
temper.

'You are off your head, Kenworthy.'

'I've been accused of that before now.'

'The woman whose character you are now tearing to
shreds is the most reliable, the sweetest-natured, the
least susceptible to mass hysteria – '

'Odd things happen to the nicest of people when they allow themselves to take on the facelessness of a mob.'

'There are no mobs in Spentlow – now.'

He looked at Horrocks and Christine, and Kenworthy did his best to signal to them to ignore the remark.

'There was a self-appointed committee, wasn't there, a sort of posse of vigilantes, set up when Spentlow was first enlivened by the threat of anarchy? Don't you at least admit that I am right about its membership?'

Dunderdale did not subside. He managed to control the untidier elements in his rage, but he was still seething.

'Moral indignation. With the best of intentions – and no harm done to a soul.'

'You believe that? No involuntary harm, even?'

'Even if there was an inkling of truth behind your insinuations, Kenworthy, it is something you would be hard put to it to prove. Besides – you have had the answer from Christine: this girl Triss and her friends – '

Christine leaned forward to protest.

'Not from me: from John – speaking out of turn. I never spoke. I told you I was far from certain – '

'Kenworthy, you will never make any sort of case against Vera Scadbolt and her friends. Emmeline Malkin is above suspicion. Geraldine Cartwright, as you yourself said, knows better than to involve herself in anything that might soil her fingers. And of the other two, I could never believe anything but their innocence.'

'It is your own innocence that I find the most touching, Vicar. And I propose to join battle. But for that I shall need Christine's co-operation and John's permission.'

CHAPTER XVIII

'Geraldine Cartwright,' Elspeth said. 'Aged fifty-four, married woman. An immigrant as far as Spentlow is concerned – came here in 1948. Husband ex-RAF, now a technical representative and away from home a lot. For which you will say, no doubt, that you don't blame him. They have two children, both grown up and left the nest: son in Zambia and daughter in Chile. Geraldine has held just about every office there is in every organization, great or small, in Spentlow. I can give you chapter and verse.'

'We can take that as read.'

'She's the only Spentlow woman whose committee work takes her outside the village: Red Cross, WVS, British Legion Women – '

'I can imagine.'

'And she's done a lot of canvassing, so far in vain, of members of the Lord Lieutenant's committee for the appointment of JP's.'

Elspeth was speaking from exhaustive notes, which she had offered Kenworthy to read. He preferred to sit dreamily whilst she picked out the highlights.

'Vera Scadbolt, maiden name Brightmore. Mother an Allsop. Married woman, forty-two. Husband an invoice clerk with the Milk Marketing Board, and they have the one daughter she told you about – a classmate of Davina's. In season she works almost full-time, as house help to Allsop's tenants. She's also worked at the school as a cleaner, kitchen help and crossing patrol – but a month's about as long as she's ever held that kind of job. It's not that she's unreliable. It's the personal relationships she can't manage. Other people start handing in their notice – and so we come to the Vicar's house-keeper.'

She turned a page, tabulated with zealous neatness.

'Doreen Malkin, aged forty-three. Born a Scadbolt, and her mother was a Brightmore. Married in 1947; her husband died in '49: of leukaemia. She became a home help for the local authority, was also in charge of the Sunday School when Dunderdale moved into his living in 1950. In 1951 she became his full-time housekeeper. There are no serious suggestions of illicit relationships between them – only ribald jokes in the lowest of company, not meant to be believed.'

'I couldn't really care whether they are to be believed or not.'

'You'll feel the same way about Alice Brightmore, then, the Colonel's help – three mornings a week, Mondays, Wednesdays and Fridays since 1955. Otherwise she has practically no income, except what she can earn cleaning for summer residents, sewing, baby-sitting, part-time help behind the post office counter in high season. Fifty-one, a spinster, dried-out, considered a prude. She'll sell raffle tickets and so on, cut sandwiches, but never gets on any committees. A mouse, in fact.'

'The night I asked for my gloves, I paid an unobtrusive visit to Sidi Barrani,' Kenworthy said.

'I noticed you packed your bedroom slippers as well.'

'I was looking for three things: I found only two of them. But I did find a home, to quote the old soldiers' phrase, as regimental as a button-stick. And the garden! If a weed had had the effrontery to appear in his rye-grass-free lawn, Colonel Noakes would emerge with a special tool, uproot weed, wipe tool clean and return it to its Dymo-labelled niche. I was looking for signs that a trowel was missing. I thought that perhaps Alice Brightmore might have borrowed one – on behalf of her friends. But there wasn't a gap in the rack. The Colonel had a small set of hand tools and still kept them in the expanded polystyrene package in which he had bought them.'

'Alice Brightmore would never have dug a trap for the Colonel!'

'I know. That's what I went to prove. Next, I wanted to see the Colonel's engagement book; as precise and legible as an order of battle. I wanted to know whether Davina had been to Sidi Barrani recently. And she had – three times – for afternoon tea. "D.S., Practise part," he had written. Finally, I looked for any evidence at all of female overnighting. I found none. Even the linen-basket had been cleared. Alice Brightmore probably did that the night she claimed she went down there to look after the Labrador. I couldn't help feeling, when I first heard that, that she'd left it a bit late in the day – '

'She had been helping out in the Hall that night, and if I know anything at all about my fellow woman, I know that Alice Brightmore wouldn't – '

'That's something that I never would claim to know. But maybe she didn't. Maybe Colonel Noakes was hung-up and virginal. I don't think now that it matters much. What does matter is that if it was only her fantasy that was threatened, even if it was only the reputation of her Commanding Officer that was at stake, it might have been enough to set her at Davina's throat.'

'Alice Brightmore!'

'Alice Brightmore out one dark night with the rest of the girls.'

Elspeth made a dramatic effort to show that she was still in command of her patience.

'Shall I go on?'

'Please do.'

'Emmeline Malkin, née Allsop. Aged forty-eight. Husband aged sixty-seven, retired farm-worker, has osteo-arthritis. Has been domestic help at Dogtooth Farm since 1955, 8.30 a.m. to midday daily, also Tuesday afternoons for the ironing. Her nocturnal

movements are well known in the village: Tuesdays and
Saturdays she spends the night at the farm, but crosses
the village only under cover of darkness.'

'Well done! And all these women have one thing in
common. They're either without men, or have the sort of
man who leaves them in need of supplementary
benefits.'

'You are disgusting, Simon.'

'But realistic.'

'Surely you see that Emmeline Malkin would never
have done anything to jeopardize Jesse Allsop. She's
only waiting for her husband to die.'

'You really think of Jesse as a marrying type?'

'She evidently does.'

'But maybe she wanted to punish him.'

'By dumping Davina's body on his doorstep? Simon—'

'I've said it before, I'll say it again – once people start
working in gangs – '

Elspeth sighed.

'Have it your own way. And you're determined to ex-
ploit Christine?'

'And myself. The bait has to be big enough. I'm determined to make that lot operate again.'

'They won't. Especially if they're as guilty as you
think.'

'We shall see.'

Elspeth tidied up her notes, put a paper-clip on them
and handed them to him. He folded them and put them
away between the pages of the bulky notebook that came
with him even on holiday.

'I'm sorry to say, Simon, that for once I have no confidence in you at all.'

'I'm sorry. I'm going to force battle, and your confidence is something I could have done with. I also need
your understanding.'

'You know you have that. You've asked Christine here
for half past ten?'

'Or thereabouts, I said.'

'And you want me out of the way?'

'That's putting it harshly.'

'It's putting it as it is. And Mrs Scadbolt?'

'Is to see what I want her to see.'

'I wish you joy of it. I'll get rid of the breakfast things for you.'

Christine had been booked for roughly ten thirty. She had still not appeared by ten minutes to eleven. Mrs Scadbolt was knocking about noisily upstairs. Kenworthy had gone back to Trollope and was turning the page at regular intervals. At five minutes to eleven there was a tap on the panel of the front door. Kenworthy went to open it and found himself face to face with Dunderdale, the vicar's cloak swaying gently behind him. Behind the cloak there was autumn sunshine on the stone outlines of the village, giving the cottages an unfamiliar, slightly incongruous look.

Dunderdale smiled, a forced smile. Kenworthy asked him in.

'I've been talking to my housekeeper.'

Kenworthy folded a slip of paper and slid it between the pages of his novel.

'A man of your experience, Kenworthy, must surely see in a single glance that Doreen Malkin is a humble, dutiful, sweet-natured, unimaginative – '

'All of that,' Kenworthy said, 'I have never doubted.'

'She has told me the truth.'

He looked at Kenworthy, expecting some help in getting his narrative launched. Kenworthy inclined his head to one side.

'But of course, you know the truth already. You know exactly who was in the group that beat Davina with nettles. At least, you almost do.'

Kenworthy appeared to be looking at him without blinking.

'My housekeeper was one of them.'

'Humble, sweet-natured,' Kenworthy mumbled. Dunderdale was riled by the sarcasm.

'Yes – humble and sweet-natured. I expect that there were humble and sweet-natured men in the crowd that howled for Barabbas.'

'Crowd psychology has a lot to answer for.'

'From their own point of view,' Dunderdale pleaded, 'they had plenty to be angry about – or thought they had, with Geraldine Cartwright moulding the bullets of moral indignation, and Vera Scadbolt aching to lead the firing of them. There was Emmeline bitterly resenting the attentions that Davina had been paying to Jesse; Alice Brightmore seething because she was making a fool of the Colonel. Doreen Malkin, rightly or wrongly, was scandalized because she thought that even I had lost my sense of proportion over the girl.'

Dunderdale paused. Kenworthy did not come to his rescue.

'Yet perhaps it is as well that they set out to trail Davina, the night she walked the brink with Kevin O'Shea. They arrived on the scene only just in time. Davina could never have defended herself.'

'Where was this?'

'In a shrubbery at the Grange. And here is something that you did not know, Kenworthy; Davina and the Irishman came down amongst the trees from the direction of the house. And behind, stalking them, was the girl everybody calls Triss: the one who had most to lose if O'Shea chose to transfer his affections. He and Davina came tripping down a slope, heading towards a mossy little corner that's a standing joke amongst everyone who knows the outskirts of this village. But when O'Shea pushed the girl down to the ground, it was at once obvious that this was to be no "debonair and gentle tale of love and languishment". It was then that the women struck, and Triss, coming in at an angle, struck too. At first it was simply a question of wrenching the couple apart: O'Shea fled, but Davina fought like a she-cat: they had to restrain her. But for that she might have escaped the beating. But her clothing was torn from her back, and it was when Vera Scadbolt caught sight of the bare flesh that she seized the first nettle.'

Upstairs, Mrs Scadbolt was knocking her broom against a skirtingboard as if she harboured ill-feeling against the very fabric of the house.

'But let me make this clear, Kenworthy. That incident was the sum total of Doreen Malkin's involvement. She was – and is – thoroughly ashamed of herself. She has never been able to erase that image from her mind. Though she did not actually herself strike the girl, she had gone so far as to uproot a nettle – '

'And she was extremely upset when she told you all this?'

'In the last throes of distress.'

'So upset that she made a couple of very bad mistakes in the telling of it,' Kenworthy said.

Dunderdale looked at him with undisguised anxiety.

'She told you that Alice Brightmore had joined in the episode of the nettles because Davina had been importuning the Colonel? But that was last August. Surely it was only with the beginnings of your play that the girl started visiting Noakes?'

Dunderdale frowned, racking his brain for an explanation.

'In other words, Dunderdale, your Doreen Malkin is getting mixed up between two occasions. She is thinking, too, of the events of that Friday night.'

'In which she did not participate at all.'

'But she does not deny that there *were* events – '

'She knew that Geraldine Cartwright had been talking to Vera Scadbolt again. About *you*, this time, and the ass they thought you were about to make of yourself over Davina. All they were going to do was spy on you, Vera

Scadbolt and some of the others.'

'*Some* of the others?'

'Doreen Malkin steered clear. She had stayed in the Hall late that night, putting the finishing touches to costumes. When we broke up she kept out of the way of the others. She cycled home alone. And for my part I cannot believe that Alice Brightmore either – '

'What you are saying is that it suits your prejudices for only two women to have been involved: Vera Scadbolt and Jesse Allsop's mistress.'

'It certainly seems – '

'It can't be true,' Kenworthy said. 'Your housekeeper cannot escape involvement.'

'I don't know on what you base that.'

'On Davina Stott's script,' Kenworthy said. 'It had got back into John Horrocks's possession. I found it up at the Grange.'

'No mystery there. I gave it to him personally.'

'That is what I was told. And how did you get hold of it?'

Dunderdale began to look concerned again.

'Doreen Malkin gave it to me. She had picked it up in the Hall when she was tidying up the next day. I expect that in all the excitement, and being escorted home by you, Davina had forgotten it.'

'She had not. She had it under her arm as we walked across the Green. She still had it with her when I left her at the gate of the bungalow. And I found a few of the bottom sheets in the very same shrubbery at the Grange that we have just been talking about. I told you that Doreen Malkin made *two* bad mistakes.'

'I am sure that there is an innocent explanation. I must have another talk with her.'

'Better you than Gleed,' Kenworthy said, and then, as Dunderdale was about to plunge them into a new inquest into the whole argument, he changed the subject with a sudden burst of apparent cheerfulness.

'What do you really make of John Horrocks, Vicar? I mean objectively, and stripping the facts of your pious hopes.'

'John Horrocks? A worthy soul, who has rapidly become unmixed since he settled here and got caught up in this teaching job. A strange mixture of moderation and madness when he first came here. Aesthetically sensitive, product of comprehensive sixth form and campus university; developed a social conscience and then went to war with the wrong enemies – alongside the wrong allies. I've wondered all along how obstinate the death-throes of his idealism would be. I'd like to think he was helped by his work on the play. It canalized him towards more balanced things. Of course, he has been besotted with Christine. He must surely have seen through the inanity of these fanatics – but Christine was uncompromisingly committed – sincerely if mistakenly.'

'The change that's come over her, since this new acting job – '

'Is scarcely believable? It's believable enough, Kenworthy, if you know the background. Middle-class, went to drama school against the wishes of both parents, couldn't make the grade when she got there. Rebelled – ineffectively – in the usual way. Went to pieces. Saved only by the devotion of John Horrocks – '

It was now a quarter to twelve. Another knock at the door, and this time it was Christine, an hour and a quarter late. Dunderdale was quick to spot that Kenworthy had something in hand, and lost no time in moving himself back to the vicarage.

She was looking pale and uncertain, her eyes nervously scanning Kenworthy's face. But at least she had made some concessions: it was the first time he had ever seen her in a skirt: a worn length of blue denim that had been made up from something unpicked. But at least it represented an effort. Beneath it she had shapely legs, bare and a little goosefleshy. She had washed and tidied her hair, but still put her fingers up at intervals as if to wipe it out of her eyes.

He stepped aside from the door and heartily asked her in. She preceded him into the shabby living-room.

'Make yourself at home. Take a good look at the fruits of a lifetime of bourgeois log-rolling.'

She laughed, not genuinely, but because it was expected of her. She sat down uncomfortably, too near to the edge of the sofa.

'Mr Kenworthy, I'm not at all certain what it is you want me to do.'

'Follow your nose. Be yourself.'

'It's going to seem strange.'

'What? Being yourself?'

'I don't mean that. Not exactly.'

She leaned her head back, closed her eyes, looked exceedingly tired.

'What, then – exactly?'

'Oh, I don't know how to explain it. Being on your side – '

'You've changed a lot – in a short space of time.'

'Have I? You, as a stranger, must notice that. Yes, I know I have. I've been liberated, that's why. If only it will last.'

'Surely it's up to you to make it last?'

'You don't really know the first thing about me, do you?' she said.

'Only what I can guess. And perhaps I've guessed wrong.'

'Go on, then – what have you guessed?'

She had opened her eyes again now, wide, and was looking into his face with frank and searching curiosity.

'That at some time or other you lit out on your own. Against all advice. And then made a mess of things.'

She acknowledged the truth of this gravely. 'Want the details?'

'If you can bear to delve.'

And she began to talk, jerkily at first, gathering confidence as she went along.

'Sevenoaks: what a background! Father Leadenhall Street on the 8.17. Mother a Weight Watcher who breeds King Charles Spaniels. I didn't do a stroke of work in my last year in the sixth – wasn't even on the school premises half the time. I leaned over backwards to get low grades in my A levels – I had to – I'd already got a provisional university place, and didn't want it at any price. That was my mother's doing. It had to be university or bust – because of my cousins. Acting was out; but I'd been Vicky in a school production of *These Glorious Years*. My father wouldn't hear of drama school. As far as he's concerned, all actresses are Zola's Nana. Mother, I think, was in two minds when I did get my place at RADA. But she couldn't see the gap between bottom and top. And Papa stuck to his guns – refused to make my money up. The mean bastard, he has plenty. I had to make do with the barest of grants. Please don't think that's what cracked me up. I got by.'

She leaned back into the sofa, looking at Kenworthy as if she were speaking from the depths of an immense physical weariness.

'I got by in the survival stakes, but when it came to acting, I was suddenly up against God knows what blockages. I just couldn't do it any more; couldn't face the footlights; couldn't learn lines. They gave me a part in an end-of-term show and I made a howling mess of it. I had no confidence; the part was far removed from me, anyway. I tried to carry the first night off by going on high.'

She remembered it with convincing revulsion.

'I don't suppose you've ever been on an LSD trip?'

'A privilege I've always denied myself,' Kenworthy said.

'I made such a bestial exhibition of myself that I had

to run away from it. That was when John found me. He was just coming out of college himself, piddling about with these anarchists. I went for anarchy in a big way – was into it far deeper than John ever was. He was marvellous. He held on to me. Steered me. Hung on to his patience, waiting for the moment to be ripe. Now, thanks to the new jobs he's got for us both, I know I can do what I'd given up hope of.'

Again the impression of last-ditch fatigue; she was struggling – and only just winning.

'John had not told me he had applied for the jobs in the school workshop drama. Ben Archer was booked to come out and see us in the normal course of rehearsals. When the play was cancelled John put on our demonstration solo. Of course, the TV boys made the most of it. Yet it hasn't been broadcast yet, has it?'

'I expect they keep things in reserve, sometimes, for when the news of the day's a bit dull.'

'My God! I hope they never do it.'

'Why not?'

'I couldn't bear to see it.'

'But you did it so well.'

'You can hardly describe it as being in the best of taste, can you?'

Mrs Scadbolt on the stairs, her pail clanking, her broom punishing the treads. Kenworthy stretched out his arm so that it ran along the back of the sofa behind Christine's head.

'You won't mind if I go a quarter of an hour early, sir? My husband was going to the dentist this morning, so he'll be home to an early dinner.'

Kenworthy stood up, took money out of his wallet to pay her. There was a shortage of small change between them, so he told her to keep the balance. When she left, Christine was laughing.

'What a ghastly woman!'

He went on with their talk as if uninterrupted.

'But now, surely, that you've got the thing over, you know you can go on to higher things?'

'I hope so. My God, how I hope so! For John's sake.'

'He hadn't thought of conscripting you into *The Anathema Stone* at an earlier stage?'

'I wouldn't do it. Half of me badly wanted to be Gertrude. The other half shied away. Besides, I knew how badly he wanted Davina in the part – because of its therapeutic value to her. That let me conveniently out.'

'Didn't you sometimes feel just a little bit jealous of her?'

'Oh, God, Mr Kenworthy – what are you suggesting?'

And Kenworthy laughed, as if he had suddenly seen the joke of the century.

'That would be a turn-up: replacing someone in amateur dramatics as a motive for murder. I expect it's been done: in paperback.'

'I still don't really get it. What is it you want me to do?'

'Just come and be seen around with me. Be with me when I pay a few calls. Come for a few country walks – taking care we are seen by the right people. Especially a certain bunch of ghastly women.'

'What good is that going to do?'

'I'm hoping it will get them up to some of their old tricks again.'

She nodded thoughtfully as if, in spite of her own reasoning, she was trying to see his point of view.

'Do you really think that this hideous crew were at the bottom of all this?'

'Somebody was. And they were about.'

'Then surely they'll take good care to remain above suspicion?'

'That depends how strongly we can tempt them. And how weak is the weakest link. One or two of them are sentimental souls. I propose to get them pretty horribly confused.'

'Is this the sort of way in which you usually tackle a case?'

'When I can get the right sort of help.'

He put his hand over hers.

'I've got a feeling we might even enjoy it.'

CHAPTER XIX

When Mrs Scabbolt came round to the back door the next morning, the Kenworthys were hammer-and-tonging it.

'I suppose it's your age, and a woman ought to be prepared for it. But this is the second time in three weeks.'

'I just happened to pass the time of day with the girl.'

'Fiddlesticks!'

'You sound like something out of a nineteenth-century novel.'

'I don't care what century a woman lives in. She ought to be free from this kind of humiliation.'

'If you're going to feel humiliated every time I speak to a pretty girl – '

'Pretty!'

Then Mrs Scadbolt was in the room, tying the tapes of her apron – and the Kenworthys were talking amicably about getting seats for a West End play the week after next.

'Oh – Mrs Scadbolt – I knew there was something I wanted to ask you. You're a close friend of Alice Brightmore's, aren't you? Has she ever said anything to you about finding a copy of the play script lying about in the lane, perhaps on the Stotts' bungalow wall, when she was on her way to or from the Colonel's cottage?'

Mrs Scadbolt looked at him with unusual intensity.

'No, Mr Kenworthy. Nothing like that. The only copy of the play I know anything about is one that Doreen

Malkin happened to mention. When we went to clear up in the Hall, after the play was cancelled, she found it on a corner of the stage, and passed it on to Mr Dunderdale.'

'Ah!'

The weather had hit one of those anti-cyclonic phases that create belated autumnal summers with fanciful names. Elspeth having said (within earshot of Mrs Scadbolt) that she had done enough walking for a lifetime, Kenworthy went out that afternoon alone, following a fieldtrack that skirted one of Jesse Allsop's walls.

Christine was waiting for him by one of the lower corners of the Grange grounds: jeans and an old beige sweater now, with her hair swept back from her forehead and secured in a pony-tail by a tortoiseshell clip. They followed a path down through a neck of woodland, along a shallow declivity scattered with mossy stones. He started a conversation about the effect on an actress's personality of a long run in a part inimical to her true self. Christine was of the opinion that some women could weather it, but she couldn't.

Once, they came within sight of a labourer forking manure from a trailer. Then Kenworthy took Christine's hand and they walked for some fifty yards along an exposed skyline, gently swinging their arms. But the moment they were out of the stranger's line of vision, Kenworthy dropped her hand again.

'I thought you were just beginning to enjoy yourself,' she said.

'The most important thing in part-playing is to remember that it is only a part.'

'Some actors do better when they sink themselves wholeheartedly into it.'

'Like Davina with Gertrude?'

'That child could r't act. A shaft of marvellous intuition now and then; but no discipline.'

At another point, where Kenworthy had let her get a few yards ahead of him along a narrow ridge, Christine turned round to find he had lagged a considerable way behind her, stooping over a hollow pock-marked with the denudations of a rabbit warren.

'Found something?'

He had obviously just slipped something into his pocket, but dissimulated shamelessly.

'I thought I had. False alarm.'

'Never off-duty, are you?'

'I am always fascinated by any tract of country where something untoward has happened. A man has passed by. There are traces as clear as a cinematograph film; if only you can damned well see them.'

'And what happened here?'

'For the last twenty minutes we have been following the route along which Davina's body was carried.'

She gave a little shudder; perhaps theatrical.

'I didn't know that. I never gave it much thought.'

'The spot where I stopped just now was one of the places where they rested the body.'

'How can you possibly know that?'

'They would, in such a spot, wouldn't they – so naturally?'

'Can't you ever take your mind off that horrible business?'

'About my only hope of that would be if it had never happened.'

But a little while later she came back to it herself.

'What makes you so certain that it was up at our place that it happened?'

'Something I found on the muck-heap in your shrubbery.'

'There's all manner of stuff there. From generations of squatters and campers.'

'Not camping out with the last few pages of Davina's script.'

'But what was she doing up there?' she asked after a long interval.

'Locked out of home. Wanted a night's lodging. She'd had one before. Many times. Hadn't she?'

'Not since that business with Kevin O'Shea and the nettles. She'd kept strictly away.'

'But on this particular night, she was in desperate straits. Those women were after her again. As I'm hoping, within a few days, they'll be after us too.'

'I don't see that. Surely, if they're the guilty parties, they'll give us a wide berth.'

'Maybe. But if murderers were all reasonable people, I doubt if I'd ever have broken a case.'

They were coming now to the edges of the Dogtooth yard, though she did not seem to recognize the place. When Kenworthy pointed it out to her, she said that she had no first-hand knowledge of this part of the village – and registered another moment of revulsion.

'But you must recognize it from the stage set?'

'I do now. Those painters did a marvellous job. But we're not going *in*, are we?'

'I thought perhaps you'd be interested in seeing.'

'I'm not interested in anything so horrible. How any man can do a job like yours – '

'Mainly because I do find it so horrible, I think. Would you like to stay here, then? There's a brief piece of business I want to do with Jesse Allsop.'

She did go with him, making appropriate gestures of distaste as crucial angles caught her eye. The gap left by the Anathema Stone had now been tidied up. The block and tackle had been removed. There was a concrete-mixer standing in the yard, and boards had been put in position for the laying of a new step.

'At least Jesse Allsop is determined to alter the image.'

Allsop was putting paper away after another after-noon of semi-laborious officework: still the same figure in worn, sober suiting, with ashen cheeks and immaculately groomed hair. But there was a certain vacancy of vision about him, as if he took Kenworthy for granted without really acknowledging who he was. And he barely seemed to notice Christine at all.

'I'll tell you what it is,' Kenworthy said. 'I've been trying desperately to get a holiday up here, and wherever I turn it all comes unglued. I thought that maybe the spring would be the time to come – in May, perhaps, when the buds are breaking on the ash, and the hayfields are a-shimmer with lady-smocks.'

If Jesse Allsop had any spirit of poetry in him it was untouched by Kenworthy's moment of transport.

'So I thought that maybe one of your caravans – if you'd be so kind as to lend me a key, so I can just have a look at one.'

Allsop went unenthusiastically to a cash-box and detached a key from a ring.

'Number sixty-nine would suit you as well as any. But you'd better lose no time in letting me have a deposit. There's not much left begging for May.'

'Thank you, Jesse. You won't mind if I hang on to this for a day or two? My wife will have to see it, too.'

Kenworthy took Christine to look at the caravan. It was modern, by Jesse's standards; even had a built-in shower, heated by Calor gas. Christine showed a suitably feminine interest in the amenities.

'This really would be rather nice – hayfields and May-time and all.'

'I had in mind a night out for us two. That ought to rouse the local moralists.'

'You don't believe in half-measures, do you?'

'I see no difficulty. Elspeth trusts me. She knows the nature of the enquiry. Your John has been marvellously co-operative up to now. In the interests, of course, purely of investigation – '

'You know,' she said, 'I don't understand you. Some-

times I think you're a slow worker. Then you take me by
storm.'

He put his arm about her shoulders, though there
were no spectators on hand to impress.

'We shan't hobble Mrs Scadbolt unless we really give
her something to talk about.'

There was another lingering hand-hold, just out of
sight of his cottage, as they were saying goodbye – and
Mrs Geraldine Cartwright was cramming herself into
her Mini outside the grocery.

Then Kenworthy made a suggestion for the next day
at which Christine demurred.

'Oh, no! Please excuse me from that, I implore you.'

'I *must* go there. And I must have a chaperon.'

'Then take a woman police officer, for God's sake.'

'I can't do that. I'm not even supposed to be meddling
in the case.'

'Then take your wife.'

'Things are reaching the stage where she doesn't want
to know about this case any more.'

'Then take Mrs Scadbolt! Take anyone you like. But
please spare me!'

'You ought to learn to be objective.'

'Why should I? I'm not training to be a policeman.'

'I don't know what you're getting so worried about.'

'I just can't bear to see human suffering.'

'Isn't that just what an actress does need to see?'

CHAPTER XX

Christine came. For the second time in three days she
was late for their date – so late that Kenworthy could
scarcely have been expected to wait for her – and in a
public place at that.

He did wait, on a wooden bench on the Green that had

been installed in memory of some village benefactor or other. Normally it was occupied by pipe-smoking old men who sat and passed three or four comments to the hour. But the presence of Kenworthy had somehow caused this passive committee to absent itself this morning. So Kenworthy sat smoking, picking his way through an elementary newspaper crossword, and enjoying what might well be the last of the season's sunshine.

When Christine did come down the hill from the Grange, she came at a fast stride, with her body leaning forward, as if it would assuage her conscience for her eyebrows and chin to arrive a fraction of time before the rest of her.

Before she saw him, Kenworthy got up off the bench and slipped unobtrusively into the shadow of one of the trees on the Green. He was thus able to observe the anxiety with which she scanned the corner on which they had arranged to meet. He slipped out obliquely behind her, was able to startle her with his hand under her elbow.

'I was beginning to think you had had second thoughts.'

'I all but did. I am sorry. I was awake half the night, dreading it. But you were right in what you said yesterday. I must learn to face up to things like this. However I feel about it, it's fifty times worse for that poor woman.'

Kenworthy led her past fields of vacant caravans and dispirited store cattle to the Stotts' home. From the state of the lawn it looked as if someone had been making an effort to infuse new order into the place. But not with signal success: everything seemed to have been started, nothing finished. A pile of sere leaves had been swept up to the edge of the untrimmed lawn, but nothing had so far been done to dispose of them. When Kenworthy rang the bell, there was the clumsy manipulation of a chain in its socket before the latch was turned. Something had been done to dust and tidy up in the hall. There was a smell of fresh furniture polish, and the webs had been cleaned from about the Pre-Raphaelite lantern.

It was Donald Stott who opened the door to them – a man of about Kenworthy's age, though looking younger at first sight, because grey hair had so far spared him, and he affected the hairstyle and casual wear of a man fifteen years younger than himself. That was at first sight; at second sight he was a tired and disabused man, who tried with his executive smile and vigorous handshake to belie his fundamental unrest.

He took them into the front room where, again, the motions of putting things to rights had been gone through: dust had been taken off picture frames; the hockey stick and broken-stringed guitar had been removed. But the plug had still not been replaced on the bar fire, though the bits and pieces lay in the hearth.

'Diana will be with us in a minute or two. I'll fix this in a jiffy.'

'No – please let me do it. It will amuse me no end.'

So, while Stott went back to his wife, Kenworthy squatted on the floor and began screwing in screws and tucking in loose ends of wire with the blunt end of his smoker's knife.

'Pathetic, isn't it?' he said to Christine, who was sitting with no effort at comfort on the edge of a fireside chair. 'It makes you want to do something more for the bourgeoisie than just liquidate their building societies, doesn't it?'

'Pathetic's the word for it. This was all that poor girl had to come home to?'

'No. Her bedroom was surely her spiritual centre. That's something I still have to see – and I'm longing to –'

It was an overspilled ten minutes before Stott came back with the coffee and his wife. By then Kenworthy had the electric fire going, with a decade of dust scorching out of its element.

Diana Stott had put make-up on thick and fast, in a manner that somehow accentuated the very ravages that it was meant to hide. There was a distinct smell of gin as she came forward to shake hands. Stott had either postponed talk of a new drying-out or was tapering her off with a generous margin.

'Mrs Horrocks – how can I thank you enough for all that you and your husband tried to do for Davina?'

And, 'I'm sorry I was so inarticulate, the day that you called, Mr Kenworthy. I just couldn't make myself plainer. I can only blame myself for all that has happened.'

'Mrs Stott, you must not do that. You were not to foresee – '

'But I *did* foresee. Didn't I try to tell you?'

She started to cry, and Stott came forward, busily and uselessly, to try to comfort her. He looked round apologetically at Kenworthy and Christine, and at last managed to get his wife on her feet and out of the room. Kenworthy beckoned to Christine and stepped quietly out into the hall, pushing open first the door of a lavatory, then of a broom-cupboard, and finally of the room that had been Davina's retreat.

There were faded rectangles of wallpaper where posters had been unpinned: pop idols and a Toulouse-Lautrec, now lying in tattered rolls on the threadbare coverlet of a divan bed. Books and long-playing records had been stacked on a window-sill. Kenworthy picked up one or two casually, but made no attempt at exhaustive inspection: an early Beatles sleeve, Cliff Richard and the Shadows, a school prize Shakespeare, a well-thumbed anthology of lyric verse from an earlier school.

'Pretty well any girl, anywhere – ' Kenworthy said. 'Give or take the odd pop star – at any time in modern history.'

They went into the kitchen, and it was there that Stott came to them, as Kenworthy was in the act of examining the chain on the inside of the back door. The paint on the metalwork was chipped and worn.

'She had both doors on the chain that Friday night?' Kenworthy asked.

'That's one of the things that's preying on her mind,' Stott said. 'She was too drunk to know what she was doing, but of course that's neither excuse nor consolation. She insists that it was the last thing she remembers doing – in a fit of hopeless rage.'

'Was Davina often locked out?'

'It had happened before, I'm afraid. Davina had her own key, but the chain had to defeat her.'

'So where did she usually go when that happened?'

Stott simply looked disconsolate.

'My God – if only I'd stayed – '

'Do you think you could really have prevented a tragedy? It had to come sooner or later.'

'At least I'd have tried. Mr Kenworthy: you must know what we are asking ourselves. Where did we go wrong?'

'You didn't go wrong, Mr Stott. It was not you who made Davina as she was. That was God's work.'

'If only we'd managed her differently.'

'I wouldn't have fancied *my* chances,' Kenworthy said.

He and Christine were silent until they were almost back in the village.

'At least they'll try,' Kenworthy said. 'They're all set for another attempt. I wouldn't put my hopes any higher than that.'

Christine found nothing to say to this.

'You know what I can't help thinking? Whoever killed Davina Stott may possibly have done a good turn to three people: her father, her mother, and perhaps even Davina herself.'

'And you really think that's a sensible argument?'
Christine asked him.

'Of course not.'

Then his tone suddenly brightened.

'Christine: previously, when Davina was locked out –
where do you think she spent the night?'

'How do I know? The vicar's? That farmer? She certainly did not come to the Grange.'

'You're sure of that? Could she not have crept in
without your knowledge? It's a big enough place – she
could have got in with collusion; perhaps even without
it.'

'Whose collusion? What are you talking about? It certainly never came to my knowledge.'

As he left her, there were this time no special endear-
ments for the sake of bystanders. But any bystander –
and there were a few – must have been struck by the
spirit of understanding between the pair.

CHAPTER XXI

'The forces are gathering.'

It was Saturday, the last whole day of the Kenworthys' stay in Spentlow. Tonight would have seen the
last performance of *The Anathema Stone*. Even their car (a
Cortina, an old friend, 150,000 miles on the clock) was
parked outside the cottage. The contents of its glove
pocket – the Guildford section of the one-inch map, a
Reader's Digest circular that had arrived once just as they
were leaving the house – had come back to them like
some relics of a forgotten world. But it was beyond the
car that Elspeth was looking, to where Mrs Scadbolt,
holding upright an ancient high-framed bicycle, was
talking to Emmeline Malkin. And a few moments later
they were joined by Alice Brightmore and Doreen

Malkin, who had come together out of the grocer's shop.

'Are your ears burning, Simon?'

He made some vacant sign with his head, and went on with his packing.

'Don't forget that you still have to return the key of the caravan.'

That was a subject that had barely been mentioned between them.

'I may still be needing it,' he said casually.

'Still living in hope, are you?'

'Gleed knows what I'm up to. He knows we go home in the morning. If he wants to play it my way – and he said he did emphatically enough – he knows he has to move himself.'

'Perhaps he prefers to wait until he has the field to himself.'

'I'd not blame him for that. But I don't think he'd say one thing and mean another.'

The group of women were now moving off together towards the small unfinished close of modern houses that had not been Jesse Allsop's most famous success in the sphere of development.

'To Geraldine Cartwright's,' Elspeth said. 'They must be feeling as frustrated as you are.'

Kenworthy made a third attempt to close the lid of a case.

'These things will have to go on the back seat.'

'I don't even know what you'd hoped to gain by this stunt, anyway. At least, I hope I don't – '

She was being teasing and non-vindictive, but perhaps not altogether uninvolved.

'Confession,' Kenworthy answered factually. 'As I see it, there may be one witness who'll turn Queen's Evidence. All the rest will be inadmissible hearsay. The jury would be left weighing one woman's word against another. And even if that were good enough for Gleed, his superiors would surely want something better.

Added to which, for the sake of my own certainty – '

'But which witness? Doreen Malkin? Alice Brightmore? Why not both of them?'

'Because I think that only two women were in on the fatal attack.'

'Oh, for heaven's sake, Simon, leave *my* clothes to *me* – And you're still hoping to prove that by a night in a trailer with Christine?'

'I'd had something of that sort in mind. But as you say, time's running thin – '

But not so thin as that. The Kenworthys finished their packing, all but what had to be left to the Sunday morning. They had decided not to spend the rest of today in Spentlow, but to use their renewed mobility to lunch out and see something of Staffordshire: Rudyard Lake and the Roaches.

But a few minutes before midday the Spentlow constable came to the door: a young officer, with his hair neglectfully long under the back of his helmet. He handed Kenworthy a tightly-packed quarto buff envelope and Kenworthy went back into the living-room and drew out a sheaf of carbon flimsies and Photostats.

'We'll lunch out all the same,' he told Elspeth. 'But I have to go up to the Grange. And for the sake of appearances I'd better go alone.'

'Gleed?'

'Has struck oil.'

When Kenworthy let himself into the caravan, Christine was at the cooker, tickling the contents of a frying-pan with a slice: a rasher or two of bacon, a tin of baked beans, a couple of eggs, two pairs of slender sausages from a plastic pack. Fortunately there was enough Calor gas left in the container. The caravan was in the clean swept state in which it had been left at the end of the season, not tarted up yet for next year; paintwork scuffed by idle heels, burns where cigarette stubs had been put down on the edge of the Formica draining-board. Kenworthy produced a bottle of Yugoslav Riesling.

'We might as well create an air of complete dissipation.'

The cooking seemed to require Christine's full concentration. She was wearing a lavender trouser suit with widely flared trousers, a cheap blouse open at the neck.

'I don't know how hungry you are.'

'Salivating.'

'I didn't know whether you'd be able to hold yourself in check long enough to eat.'

Her tone was a mixture of cynicism and open options. She was clearly prepared to play whatever happened whichever way it came: and that without faith in anything or anyone.

She had scattered the contents of a holdall on to the cantilevered double bed: a diaphanous nightdress, a pair of new tights, still in the packet, a garishly floral patterned toilet bag that contained God knew what intimacies. Some time during the last week she must clearly have been out of the village on a shopping expedition. It was unthinkable that she had had this stuff in store during the full flush of her anarchy.

Kenworthy went to the window and pulled at a corner of the curtain, uncovering a narrow triangle of window.

'Not much point in our being here if we don't advertise the fact.'

'Whoops!'

She was no dab hand with a frying-pan. Getting an egg out intact must always have been a matter of chance for her.

'You don't seriously think that that lot are going to pay us a visit?'

'If they don't, I am wasting my time.'

'Then why waste it? Wouldn't it do for a famous policeman to be honest about what he's here for?'

Kenworthy was at the cupboard, trying to sort out a matching set of anything in the crockery line. Two grey-filmed tumblers were all he could find for the wine.

'I'm prepared to make the most of the company while I'm about it.'

He smiled at her as he might have smiled at his daughter. His attitude puzzled her. The only sort of smile she knew how to return was stagey and short-lived.

'I must say, John Horrocks is being very patient and understanding,' he said.

'He trusts you.'

'And you too?'

'Listen: I'll hear nothing against John. If it hadn't been for him, I'd have been messed up for good – been fished out by now from under some bridge with punctures all the way up my arm.'

'I dare say. But I still think he's being more trustful than many a man.'

'You're a copper, aren't you? We're on the right side of you, aren't we? We want to stay there. You can have your little bit of ultimate anarchy too, if you fancy it. Do you think we care? Do you think we own each other, the way you and your wife do? You're going away tomorrow. In any case – '

'In any case what?'

'John believes in you. He still thinks you've something up your sleeve.'

'I have something up my sleeve.'

'What, then?'

'A missing link in a chain. I know precisely what happened, the night Davina Stott was killed.'

It was uncomfortable at the folding table. There was no room for their elbows or knees, barely space for their cutlery and plates. Kenworthy filled up their glasses.

'Just the vintage for bacon and egg.'

But she ignored the sidetrack.

'I'll buy it,' she said. 'What did happen?'

Kenworthy chewed slowly.

'We'd had a late rehearsal, remember? You weren't there, but you must have got tired of waiting for John to come home.'

'He was often late home.'

'I know. He stopped off for a quick one after hours in the Recruiting Sergeant – and that often developed into several leisurely ones.'

'So what? I dare say your own wife sometimes – '

'Oh, certainly, yes. We family men try you women terribly hard. Including that night. I was down the lane with Davina Stott till a very late hour. Much to my wife's concern. Though I must confess that I did not know then how closely observed I was.'

He paused.

'Vera Scadbolt, Alice Brightmore, Emmeline Malkin: Davina and I were giving them their biggest treat of the decade. And after I'd left her I'm pretty sure they trailed her back to the Grange. And we come here to a point, my dear, on which I fear that you have been less than ingenuous with me.'

She looked at him sharply. She may not have been certain what ingenuous meant, but she did not mistake its impact.

'I don't understand you.'

'You told me that Davina had not slept at the Grange since that business with Kevin O'Shea had scared her off.'

'Nor had she – to my knowledge.'

'On the contrary, I have reason to think that she made a regular habit of it – whenever, in fact, her mother had put the door on the chain.'

'Yes, well, look, the Grange is a rambling place. We never did lock the door. There was nothing to prevent her from finding her way in.'

'Not even her fear of another mass onslaught with nettles?'

'That was done by the village women.'

'Mostly. But she did not regain her confidence without good grounds. She came in under protection, perhaps. Whose protection would that be?'

'I don't know. I don't know who'd protect her.'

'Oh, come, Christine. You do yourself less than justice. Who but John Horrocks? John – who was making it his job to protect her even from herself. He knew what she was up against, knew what her home was like, what was the muddled state of her own mind. He desperately wanted, too, to keep her out of the clutches of public welfare. Would he have denied her a bed for the night?'

'If there was anything like that going on, I knew nothing about it.'

'You mean there could be comings and goings about the landings of that dark old house at night that you might know nothing about? You mean that John would deceive you?'

'I'd be surprised if he did.'

'Or had Davina been a bone of contention between you?'

'You don't think I was jealous of her do you?'

Then Kenworthy suddenly laughed, and immediately took off the pressure.

'God – why am I talking like this? Anyone would think I was interrogating you. Sorry, Christine. I suppose it gets to be a habit with me. But I do think that something was going on – something quite simple and innocuous. Let's say, just to save misunderstanding, that nobody bothered you with it.'

She looked at him with confused comprehension.

'So let's say Davina came up to the Grange after she left me. Let's say she hung about outside, waiting for John Horrocks to come home from the pub, to give her safe entry. Let's say she was being observed from the shrubbery. Let's say the reception committee suddenly revealed themselves – and she thought she was in for

another chastisement with nettles. So what would she
do?'

'Run for it.'

'And if she was caught – fight for it. Fight like a wild
cat. Fight so she had to be restrained with more force
than anyone had set out to use. Fight with her finger-
nails, toe-caps and sharp-shod heels. Fight and have to
be held so that one of her attackers suddenly shouts,
"My God – you've killed her." And shall I tell you what
happened next, Christine?'

She was no longer interested in the food on her plate.

'I don't know why you're telling me this. As far as I am
concerned – '

'A woman found,' Kenworthy said, 'that for a moment
of time she had a dead girl not only on her hands, but in
them. She was a woman who had lost all her friends, who
was standing alone at this instant with the only other
crony who was still with her.

'What am I going to do with her? What am I going to do?'
'That's your affair. You never did know where to draw the
line.'
'You've got to help me. You've got to help me get her away from
here.'
'Why should I help you? What have you ever done for me?'
'I'll do anything you want.'

'Then came the great inspiration: Dogtooth. Carry
her down to the doorstep. Lay her across the Anathema
Stone, leave her where she had writhed hysterically in
that appalling last scene of the play. Think what a mesh
of false trails that was going to create, what a turmoil of
cross-scents and madcap old histories.

'Then the other woman stated the terrible terms for
her co-operation. Is this making sense, Christine?'

'How could I possibly know? I wasn't there.'

'Then that terrible trek down the hill, when two

women discovered that carrying a girl's body over a long distance, before rigor has set in, is something they've never practised before. They quarrelled as to who should take the ankles and who the armpits. They needed to stop more and more often to rest. Once, they stopped at the spot that I pointed out to you: in the hollow of the rabbit warren. That was where the accomplice reiterated the price of her silence; and the murderess made promises that she had no intention of keeping. Then at last they were in the yard at Dogtooth, and could turn their backs on their burden.'

Kenworthy pricked up his ears and held up his hand to silence any reply that Christine might make; not that she looked as if she had any words on her lips. He held up a finger and made her listen.

The Spentlow night was full of its own noises. A bullock came up to the caravan and snuffled round the window. But there were other sounds too in the field: voices whispering, feet dragging through long, damp grass. Christine's ears picked up the sounds too, and she listened with him. There was the scrape of a key in the lock of one of the other caravans, a man's voice and a woman's as the couple climbed in.

Kenworthy chuckled.

'There must be more duplicate keys than Jesse Allsop knows about.'

But Christine was no longer alert to any sense of the comic.

'I have no idea what you have been talking about.'

'Just let's say it was all theory. I'm sure you'll admit there's a strong element of probability in it.'

'How on earth can I know whether there is or there isn't?'

'Don't you even recognize some of the things that were said – and the stages in the journey of the corpse?'

She looked at him with round eyes. For the first time she seemed to see that she was physically trapped, wedged into her seat, his bulk between her and the door.

'It was Patricia Cave – Triss – who helped you to carry Davina down that valley. You'd been fretful that night, because John Horrocks was late from rehearsal and pub. You went out to look for him, and instead of John Horrocks, you ran into Davina, coming up through the trees, her script under her arm. I do not think that you meant to kill her. I think that the pressure of your hatred gave a strength to your fingers that simply took over. There you were, wondering what John was about, wanting him, looking forward to bed. And there was Davina, locked out again, Davina with another problem, another confession, another demand on John Horrocks's good-natured time. How often had you been robbed of John Horrocks at bed-time by the arrival of Davina with a problem? You could even picture the next morning, as had happened before: John having to wake her, to get her up, to take her down with him to catch the school bus.'

Kenworthy waited for a reaction, but there was none.

'I'm sorry: there was no school bus the next morning, was there? They were on half-term holiday. So Davina would have been able to lie in. And you weren't the only one who was about in the woods that night. Patricia Cave was also abroad, up and snooping, always nosing, wanting to know all the undercurrents. You called desperately on her for help. She made terms. She'd help carry the corpse. She would keep her mouth shut. Only you had to get out of the Grange, out of the commune, out of their lives, leaving her the clear field she had had before you came. Including a clear field with John Horrocks. But it was different in the light of morning; you knew Triss couldn't hold you to it, that she could not have said a word without admitting herself an accomplice. You hung on. Triss cut her losses, lit out the day after Gleed's raid. Gleed's minions picked her up the day before yesterday sleeping rough in an old barn off the A6, somewhere south of Manchester. And Triss has talked. I have a full copy of her statement.'

'You don't think the word of that bitch will count for anything?'

'No. I don't think that for a moment. That's why I've brought you here.'

Kenworthy was a well-built man. His body commanded the space between the girl and the exit. Her knees were jammed under the table. Her eyes glanced at the window. Short of a farm spade, with space to swing it, she could never have broken her way out. Bacon, eggs and baked beans were congealing on the plate in front of her.

'Claustrophobic, isn't it?' Kenworthy asked.

'You can keep me here all night if you want. I'm not saying another word.'

'Listen!'

The command was so sudden and firm that in spite of herself she did listen. But there was nothing to hear that meant anything to her. There was only the wind in distant restless trees, a loose-fitting clanking on one of the caravans, a bullock snorting. Kenworthy let the night fill their ears.

'You think you're going to break me down?' she said at last. 'You think I'm a romantic or something?'

'You're what the Americans call a tough cookie. In another few minutes we're going to see how tough.'

'You're a fool, Kenworthy.'

'Listen!'

Somewhere between their field and the village, the passion of a barnyard cat, the gurgle of water from a feed-pipe into a cattle trough.

'The night is never empty,' Kenworthy said.

'Bollocks.'

And then there was hardly anything to be heard beyond Kenworthy's regular breathing. It was almost an hour after they had first sat down together that they heard new sounds: something that distinctly did not belong to the setting. It was a rhythmic beat, as of metal against resonant metal; a chanting; breathless, ill-humoured and insistent. Soon it resolved itself into marching feet, accompanied by improvised percussion.

'Whore of the Beaker Folk – whore of the Grange – whore of the Beaker Folk – whore of the Grange – '

There was a barefaced, primeval self-satisfaction in the women's voices. Within a minute they were in a circle round the caravan, striking its panels with their pokers and sticks, the classical chorus of enraged rustic decency as perpetuated in folk-lore and literature.

Then a second's silence was followed by apparent consultation outside. Kenworthy got up and flung open the door on Mrs Scadbolt, a copper kettle in one hand, a brass fire-shovel in the other; behind, to her left, stood Emmeline Malkin with a dustbin lid; to her right Alice Brightmore, using saucepan lids as cymbals; behind them other pale faces, indistinguishable in the darkness.

'All right, ladies. As you know, I am not here in any official capacity. I don't think I can do better than leave her to you – '

He began to step down from the trailer, and Mrs Scadbolt squeezed past him into the space he had vacated.

'No!' from Christine. 'Mr Kenworthy, please – '

'Of course, you ladies have seen nothing of me – '

'Whore of the Beaker Folk – whore of the Grange – '

Three of the women were in the trailer now. Someone pulled Christine's hair. Vera Scadbolt was leering into her face, her crimson cheek-bones close under her eyes. Someone else tore at the neck of Christine's blouse.

Kenworthy stepped sideways and tapped on the window of the next caravan in the line. Gleed jumped down, followed by a woman officer in plain clothes.

'She'll talk. She'd put her neck into a noose to get those women off her back.'

'Quite clever,' Elspeth said, 'if a trifle circuitous. I don't really see the need for all the convolutions – except for the sake of a man in his forties who sees his youth rapidly vanishing.'

Kenworthy pulled into the verge and switched off the engine to allow passage to a milking herd.

'Far from it. She was a tough baby. Without utter breakdown, there'd be little hope of a conviction. Damn it, I wasn't even sure myself. To get a confession, I knew I would have to spend a long time with her, and that I would need a convincing cover story – one that would convince both her and everyone else in the village. So I was able to push her. I took her step by step down the track where she'd carried the corpse. I made her look at the gap where the Anathema Stone had been. I took her into Davina Stott's bedroom. Now and then she quailed, but never beyond the point at which it might not have been just another spot of theatre. And all the time there was the thought in her mind that I might really be going to swing it circumstantially on the vigilantes. Also, she was never quite sure whether I wanted her or not. Every man has his price, and she must have thought she was within my bracket.'

'There ought to be a medal struck for Mrs Scadbolt and Co.'

'They played ball. After I'd had a word with my good friend Geraldine Cartwright. But what really kept me on the *qui vive* was the constantly recurring theme of Davina's script. Christine was the one who had returned it to the Hall for Doreen Malkin to find. A bad mistake: not because it told me anything for a very long time, but because it told me so little that it preyed on my mind.'

'And what about John Horrocks now?'

'Poor devil. A hard lesson. I hope he'll learn to keep better company. He might even stand by her, as faithful spouses tell the judge. But at least they'll both have leisure to think.'

They were now descending a one-in-five gradient that called for a halt on the white line of a major road. He looked back over his shoulder at the roots of a hornbeam sprawling over lichen-covered rock.

'You know, one of these days, we ought to think of a holiday up here. Some time in the spring, when the ash-buds are breaking and there's a shimmer of lady-smocks in the hayfields.'